Humanimality is a confrontation, a hybrid monster of a book that interrogates humanity's troubled relation with its animality, *&* so its relation to animals, the earth, and ultimately the cosmos.

In driving not only many species to extinction, but also endangering its very own existence, as well as imperiling the life of the planet, homo sapiens seem to be the most foolhardy species to have evolved since the dawn of time. Will the species drive itself to extinction, or will life itself, for evolution has not ceased, bring about the demise of that species through natural selection in order to preserve the planet? If other species have come and gone since the formation of life on earth, the persisting of homo sapiens is considerably dubious.

Philosophy, religion, *&* science spiral through this book like chemicals to cross, charge, *&* finally detonate in an astonishing denouement.

Humanimality is a bastard child, a book with nothing but the logic of physics to map the ecstasy of life.

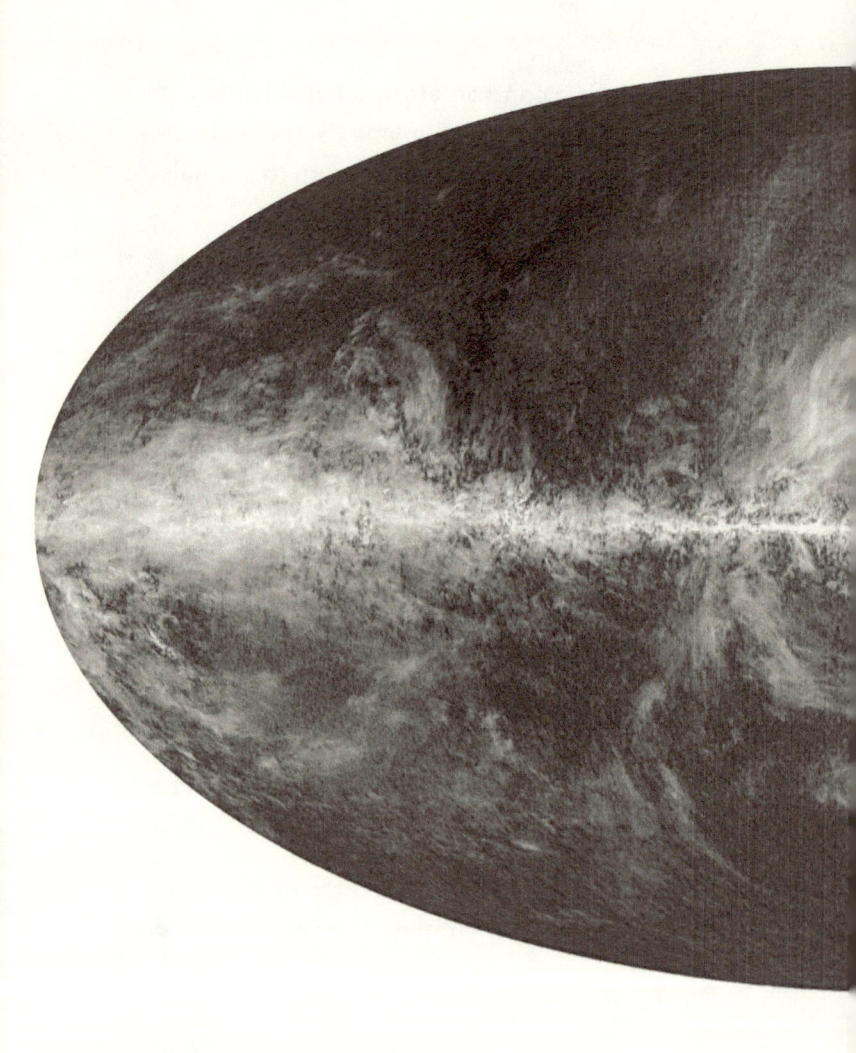

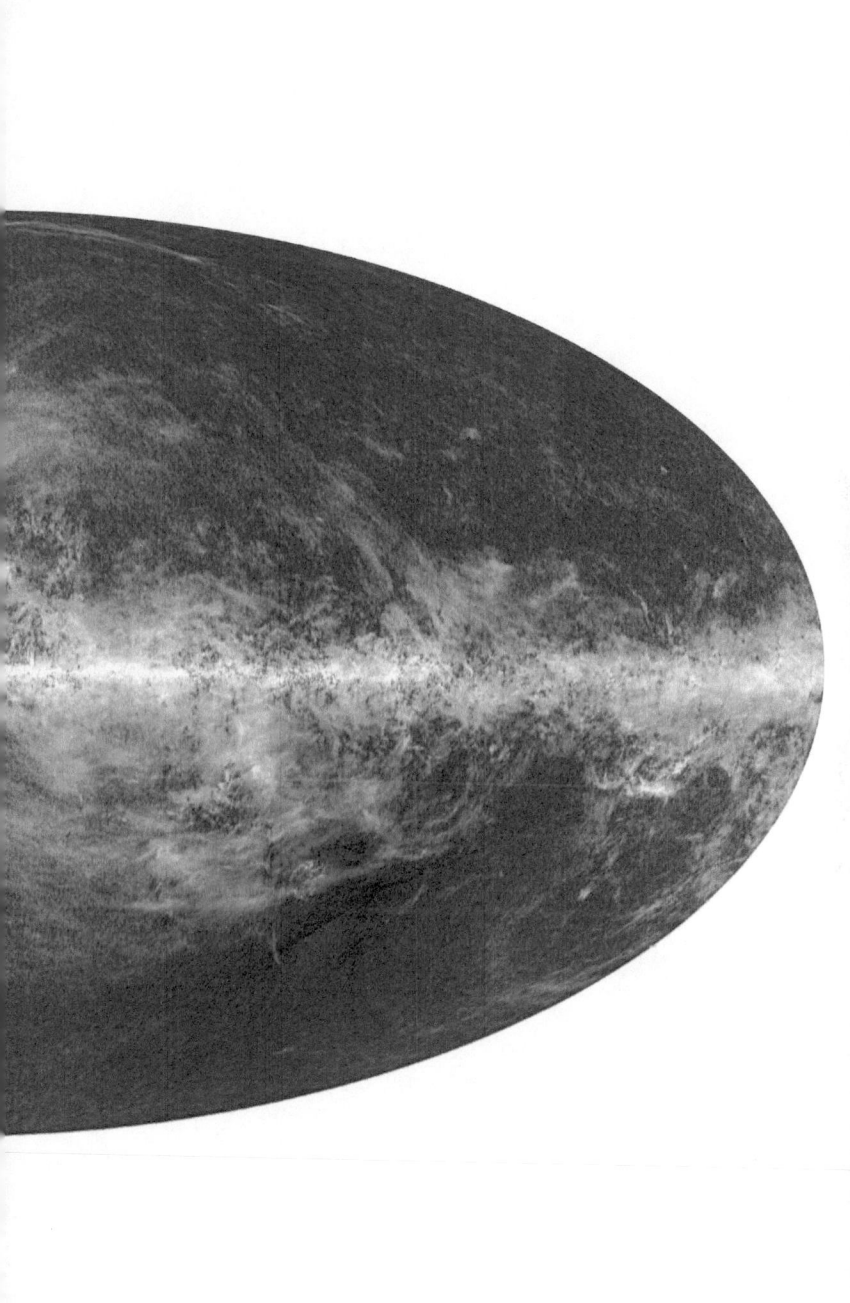

Advance Praise

Once in every century, a work of this caliber arrives. Like Diderot's *D'alembert's Dream*, or Kafka's "A Report to an Academy," Hanshe's *Humanimality* inverses comedy into tragedy, and vice versa. The result is a visceral breakdown of the word and of the flesh. In a gesture of involuting, as an undoing, the writer here reverses the spell of the civilized homo sapiens. A book as a counter-spell presents itself then (the highest degree of any writing). What remains after this extinguishing of inner terror, one that shaped humans for the past 10,000 years? There are no traces left, only a pure intensity: honest, unforgiving to oneself, unrepentant; an intense line that was always there at the foundation of all chaos and all lies and all truths and all space and all time. That is the line carved in *&* by *Humanimality*. One can only imagine what price the writer had to pay to incise this intensity. I will venture to say it anyway: a lifetime of abandonment and renunciation; refusal of all conformist sensibilities; reckless focus. No, wrong, it took millions of lifetimes condensed into a crystal of pure and alien (little known) thought procedure. That is to say, through rogue firmness a veritable dissipation of borders between the human *&* the animal is summoned here. But do not be afraid. This extinguishing is exuberant. For it is tactile, auditory, olfactory. It heightens the senses. As such, it is utterly concrete, bursting with all kinds of material forms.

Yet it might also be a dream. A hallucination wrenched from a stupor of enlightenment. Clearly we are beyond the space of literature now. The voices are inhuman *&* so is the demand to embrace them. A demand devoid of ethics, a demand for a reversal, which leads to the revival (of the earth, at dawn…)."

— Dejan Lukić

A cross between a supremely erudite *Planet of the Apes* and a lightning-swift tackle of the great books of Western civilization from the Bible *&* Ancient Greeks on, Rainer J. Hanshe's *Humanimality* is a biting (often in the literal sense) satire of everything but the cosmos, itself viewed strictly (if exuberantly) as naught but the explosive, untouched energy of the natural universe. A "mortal comedy" setting out to invert Dante's journey *&* heralding Nietzsche as its guide to a fully grounded, despiritualized realm, this highly sapient yet vibrant *&* compelling tale shreds the texts of countless thinkers and writers from Plato to Heidegger, Aeschylus to Blake and Tennyson, no matter their discipline, tribe, or creed. In a stunning array of fragmentary quotations *&* allusion after allusion, Hanshe savages the world of letters to bits so as to lay bare its part(s) in humanity's auto-destruc-tion — a catastrophe, which, left unchecked, threatens the whole of life on earth. Happily, as befits a comedy, "all" ends well. A marvelous companion piece to the author's *Dionysos Speed,* which carried readers on a dizzying jaunt through the deathly digi-sphere we're heading toward, this new philosophical novel previews the splendid primeval world we might return to, by forcefully reminding us whence and how far we've come. But do not expect any ancient or newfangled pieties here — physics reigns alone *&* only the better to perceive chaos —, for this work's assault on all lofty humanistic endeavors also engulfs itself, deploying *&* challenging, most learnedly, all varieties of long-tested thought *&* invention and the precision of an astonishing wealth of instructive, edifying words. Writing with keen poetic *&* incantatory powers, Hanshe creates a book bound to be doomed by its own rowdy logic, insofar as it is at once frightening, informative, amusing, *&* lyrical. *Humanimality* is a salty song that leaves higher beings merely laughing while gazing at the stars, consigning all gloomy ink-recorded "drop(s) of nothingness" — as Mallarmé once depicted human consciousness — safely back to sea.

— Mary Lewis Shaw, author of *The Cambridge Introduction to French Poetry and Performance in the Texts of Mallarmé: The Passage from Art to Ritual*

Humanimality

Humanimality

Directions in writing

by Rainer J. Hanshe

Contra Mundum Press   New York · London · Melbourne

Humanimality
© 2025 Rainer J. Hanshe

ISBN 9781940625775

First Contra Mundum Press
edition 2025.

I. Hanshe, Rainer J.
II. Title.

2025931909

Library of Congress
Cataloguing-in-Publication
Data

>   Hanshe, Rainer J.
>   Humanimality /
>   Rainer J. Hanshe

—1st Contra Mundum Press
    Edition

>   200 pp., 5 × 8 in.

Lacking external enemies and obstacles, and forced into the oppressive narrowness & conformity of custom, man impatiently ripped himself apart, persecuted himself, gnawed at himself, gave himself no peace & abused himself, this animal who battered himself raw on the bars of his cage & who is supposed to be 'tamed'; man, full of emptiness & torn apart with homesickness for the desert, has had to create from within himself an adventure, a torture-chamber, an unsafe & hazardous wilderness — this fool, this prisoner consumed with longing & despair, became the inventor of 'bad conscience.' With it, however, the worst & most insidious illness was introduced, one from which mankind has not yet recovered; man's sickness of man, of himself: *as the result of a forcible breach with his animal past, a simultaneous leap & fall into new situations & conditions of existence, a declaration of war against all the old instincts on which, up till then, his strength, pleasure, & formidableness had been based.*

Nietzsche, *On the Genealogy of Morality*

Shall we attain the high philosophical goal of perceiving how the divine life in man can be joined in all innocence with animal life?

Goethe

Terrorem in eos suscitare, excitare terram.

Full Speed Behind

Humanimality is an agon, a war on the tyrant of tyrants, an unfolding & dismantling of the strangest animal in the history of evolution: *homo sapiens*. The relation that such have with their animality, and thus their relation to the earth, to animals, and to the cosmos itself, is what is enacted in this hallucinatory & phantasmagoric hazard. To both usurp and subvert Dante, we might call this book a sort of *mortal comedy*. A bestial assault & transvaluation where, through twenty-four sequences, all that is divine is eviscerated to reveal it to be nothing less than an infernal disaster, a pandemic wherein festering mythologies that have usurped physics for far too long are made to finally disintegrate.

Although some of the species struggled to emerge from this perilous comedy throughout its history, despite the insights of some philosophers and scientists, it remains embroiled in it, entangled in an obscuring shadow that perhaps only animality can disperse. Born of religion & science, an ethics was forged that has shaped (*deformed*) civilization with the development of mythologies & religions, the founders of which were profoundly troubled, if not terrified, by their propinquity to the kingdom out of which they seethed. Throughout time, and especially since the emergence of the so-called great books 10,000 years ago, homo sapiens have essentially denied their consanguinity with the animal, differentiating themselves as everything from the political to the laughing to the tool-making species, but with greater knowledge and understanding of insect & animal kingdoms (not to speak of fungi, monera, plantæ, etc.), each definition suffered fracturing, as did the species itself, its question regarding its nature undermined, making it something radically ambiguous and indeterminable. The human is not a fixed, definite substance — it is something which has not only always been on the verge of erasure, but something which has also undergone actual erasure, an entity that, time & again, has had its identity, and so itself, effaced. There is no absolute biological substance to permanently ground the human. Whatever that strange species might be, it disappears as swiftly as it appears.

Before the advent of the Roman Catholic Empire, Plato famously defined man as a featherless plantigrade biped. Then in bringing forth a plucked chicken and stating, "There is Plato's man for you," Diogenes the Cynic mocked and destabilized the philosophical characterization of the species, ultimately revealing its nebulosity. Beyond the humor of the Cynic's gesture, one largely discounted as an act of sophistry, was something eerily prescient. In 2004, researchers demonstrated that chickens have the same number of protein-encoding genes as humans. If 75% of their genes are identical on average, rodent and human gene pair resemblances are even greater, being 88% identical on average, testifying to the close link between humans and animals, a seemingly undeniable fact consequent to Darwin's discoveries, but evidence is what much of the dissimulating species refutes in its reactive turn against its nature. When challenged by Diogenes, Plato was forced to redefine his term, prompting the philosopher to present evidence of the existence of nymphs and daimones. Since centaurs, satyrs, and the like don't in fact exist, man remains eerily indistinct. With each new definition philosophers and scientists wield, homo sapiens is in threat of constant slippage into non-existence, into indeterminacy, which calls to mind Diderot's question (prediction?) in *D'Alembert's Dream* that, "who knows whether this misshapen biped a mere four feet in height, which is still called man in polar regions, but which would very soon loose that name if it went just a little more misshapen, is not the image of a passing species?"

More however than any philosophical heritage, the metaphysical one is the most pestiferous, with man endowing himself with spirit, separating himself from the earth (matter), animals, and ultimately the cosmos, establishing a perilous ethics that has threatened and endangered every other form of life, from minerals to plants to atmospheres, and so the life of the species itself. Terrified of its primordial origins, terrified of animal, mineral, vegetal, terrified of the vast dark expanse of space, of meteor, star, and planet, of nebula, supernova, and black hole, of dark matter and dark energy, but most of all, terrified of its closest ancestor, the simian, the beast that it nearly is, the beast who mirrors it 98.8%, the beast who speaks to it mutely with its every knowing glance, terrified of its sublime eloquence, homo sapiens conceived of the animal as savage and founded the lie of lies. Toward the end of the Dark Ages, the phrase "ape-ware" was used to refer to deceptive or false ware, tricks.[1] The great deception or trick however lies in the human, making the phrase *homo sapien-ware* far more apt. Turning away from time, turning away from millennia of data, turning away when it was much closer to the animal, turning away from its whole archaic past, from tumults and upheavals and ice ages, turning away from ape, from earth, stone, lava, gas and carbon, through the most ingenious and astounding

---

1. Hans Kurath (ed.), *Middle English Dictionary* (1998) 309. "He [Satan] ne may do no more bot putte forþ his aped ware & þreten vs to biggen þerof."

subterfuges, the species fled fearfully into myth, creating spirit, declaring itself the offspring of a metaphysical entity (*spectral simulacrum*), a being made in its image, thereby giving itself dominion over animals and all else, establishing the plague that could lead to its end. Endowed with divine attributes, it believes its form of consciousness is superior to all others. Is the cosmos, and the earth within it and upon which we live, truly mute, or is it that the logocentric monster par excellence is but deaf to all forms of intelligence, save its own? Is language not a myopic Mobius strip within which humanity has imprisoned itself, locking out the open variability of reality, perceiving nothing but biological forms of life as life? *Prejudice of prejudices*. In fear of its own animality, in terror before the simian, the human must give itself power over insects, animals, & plants to further separate itself from a heritage that continually undermines it. Was there some moment in the ancient past, a moment when the species was much closer to its animal origins, some moment when the truth of that was too unbearable to face, that with the onset of consciousness, in the face of a universe devoid of meaning, which most of the species could not endure, it had to erase its past & establish a mythology instead of a physics?

If later the existence of feral creatures such as Homo Sylvestris put man yet further into question, so did talking parrots, laughing animals, and tool-making ones, when just over one century after the publication of Darwin's *Origin of Species*, Jane Goodall observed chimpanzees fashioning sticks into tools, affrighting the metaphysically enraptured members of the species. An event, perhaps in some way cataclysmic, that met with as much doubt as did the discovery of ancient caves such as Lascaux and Altamira. Even at as late a stage in history as the 1960s, recognizing that man was not the only tool-making animal was anathema to many believers. It was as if, even in the post-Darwinian epoch, the thought of being closely related to apes remained unnerving. Was this a truth, already proven by Darwin, that would plunge mankind into the fate Diderot predicted? Did the species fear being reduced into a kind of jabbering primate, or did it fear *the elevation of the chimpanzee*, of that species being brought ever closer to the threshold of humanity, of humanity too becoming prey, of it discovering that *To Serve Man* is not an altruistic treatise but a book of recipes?

To many, the animal is a figure of pure instinct: a savage, violent beast devoid of rationality, with all inhumane acts categorized as animalistic. In contradistinction, man is rational, sane, logical, but the Enlightenment era (and later others) demonstrated the terrors of rationality brought through instrumentalization to its logical extreme. Again and again, the species cites the first Delphic imperative, Γνῶϑι σαυτόν (*gnōthi sauton*, know thyself), but very rarely, hardly ever, the counter-balancing second imperative, μηδὲν ἄγαν (*medan agan*, nothing in excess), which warns against hubris and the contravening of boundaries. Rationality and consciousness, despite oft being majestic, seem to be perilous developments, muscles that mankind overdeveloped to its detriment, and the detriment of others. If man (**men-*) is one who has intelligence, as the species assures itself, as it asserts and proclaims, what is this intelligence it so prizes? What is this savagery of grey matter? Is it not *bhragnoic*? Is it not something broken? Is the species not all *brægenseoc*? An *ourion ōon*? Too hasty to turn all the way back into dark millennia, the impatient animal goes back only thousands of years and proclaims that it was made in the image of a deity. How riotous, a higher ape might say. Genesis, the great comedy, the great tragi-comedy — once animals discover this book, they might read it to their offspring as a moral tale, as a warning, as a sign of everything to fear in the *homo-sapien*. And they say that the adder is deaf? And that it closes its ears? The animal hearkens not to the voice of men charming for it knows what men are. It has spun its incantations to cast itself into dark caverns, into the dark abysses of its mythologies, abysses from which it has not entirely emerged — loving its darkness, it coiled up to hideth itself, to choose not to come forth, to choose to restrict and coil itself into a *homo*, into the terrifying *self-same!* It presses one ear to the ground, and it uses its hand to stop up the other, because it long ago cut off its tail and escaped as much as possible its primordial past to hide in its antediluvian one, in its comedy, in its terrifying tragedy. If the animal is savage, there are no serial killers in its kingdom, nor any arbiters of final solutions.

As the sole species that endangers its own habitat, as well as the habitats of others, what might other animals think of this strange, tyrannical creature known as the human? Will it escape its hubris? Will the self-appointed crown of creation and king of the planet overcome its fatal flaw, or will it spiral into an inevitable oblivion, one not however fated, but one that it has unconsciously engineered, yet which, in an extraordinary act of prestidigitation, it disguised as the inevitability of the historical *spirit*, or divine will.

Is the earth itself, and all species and kingdoms upon it, in danger of total annihilation, or is there a pathway out? Is the new future not out of spirit, out even of the sciences that remain bound to the ascetic ideal? Is the new future not a politics wherein humanity undergoes the most radical despiritualization, as does the earth and the cosmos, with the species recognizing itself as nothing more than animal *&* where the animal kingdom, as every other, is recognized as an integral element of *the polis of the earth*? It is into this future of animality, of plantness, of minerality, etc., where the species must proceed, for that is the only future, the only open that remains. Otherwise, natural selection will send homo sapiens spiraling into an inferno of its own making. In its place, other species will ascend and seize dominion of the earth *&* the cosmos, for evolution has yet to cease. Do not let the slowness of time deceive.

Did the species not say to itself, through the mouth of another, did it not give itself the command, "Remember ye not the former things, neither consider the things of old" (Is. 43:18)? To this willful cultivation of blindness, the animals might say, Unman the ark, *full speed behind, beyond the Big Bang!*

Consider things of old, consider antiquity, consider the millennia that preceded you.

Now, let us enter into the fiercest confrontation with animality, with the plant kingdom, with all forms of biomass. Let us enter into the mortal comedy.

Rainer J. Hanshe
7 April 2024
The eve of the Solar Eclipse

Humanimality

Between astronomical twilight & dawn, an eerie supersonic frequency provokes flights of dragonflies to halt, ascend, reverse, turn about, and soar toward the sound, then hover before the entity emitting it.

Whether it is a hologram, a fata morgana, a computerized projection, or an actual event, its movement is so accelerated that it is visible only to the 30,000 ommatidia of the insects whose mosaic vision can perceive the chaotic changing play of ambient light and full tilt motion of the phenomenon. Were a human within its vicinity, it could not witness it, even if face before it.

Transfixed by the entity, the vast swarm of dragonflies continues to hover there, an immense orb of Odonata, as if, into the very air, nature had cut a living acoustic hieroglyph.

From afar, a sleuth of black bears detect sweet, floral-honey scent molecules emerging from Ambrosia apples & wafting across what is left of their home range.

Standing on their hind legs, they sniff the air to determine the location of the fruit.

Undeterred by the sound of a human voice they hear adjacent to the scent, for the allure of the fruit is more attractive than the presence of homo sapiens, the bears begin moving in the direction of the orchard, swiftly running toward their mark.

As they pick fruit from the ground, devouring apple after apple, breaking the skin with their teeth, the flesh of the fruit releasing other flavors only they can taste, a news report sounds over a radio abandoned in the grass:

... *the mutilated body was discovered early this morning by zookeepers. Detectives said that the head of the victim had been shaved, the skin of the skull pulled tautly and neatly back, the brain showing evidence of surgical markings.*

Climbing the trees, the bears broke off the big branches of the plants and knocked more fruit to the ground, freeing the trees of their outgrowth.

Once descended, they gathered from below the fruit they were unable to reach when above.

The radio report continued:

The chest of the victim had also been sawed open, as if to display the organs for examination, folds of flesh dexterously arranged, clipped, pinned, a meticulous and careful manipulation of the body that only a skilled surgeon could have performed.

Lolling about, the bears frolicked amongst the apples, shaking more of them free from the tree, feasting upon them with delight, chomping them in half, sucking in their juices, the broadcast going on:

Shocked and terrified by this ghastly autopsy-murder, people are referring to the killer as Dr. Death. Although reluctant to divulge any details, detectives revealed that the dissected body was not a corpse, but a freshly killed person. The zookeeper was quoted as saying only an evil animal could've done something so sick.

At this moment, no motive has been determined for the gruesome autopsy-murder, the identity of the victim has not been verified, and no missing persons cases have been filed to date. No clues have been discovered enabling detectives to determine who may have committed the crime, but they are visiting local hospitals to see if any surgical instruments are missing, or have been stolen.

Surgeons remain the prime suspects, and the personal histories of local doctors are being investigated. The Surgical Association has denounced the crime and stated that if in fact the killer is a doctor they will perman—

The radio cut out then, one of the bears unknowingly crushing its speaker as she meandered about, the animals continuing to savor the apples, particularly because of their lack of tartness & the subtle, earthy banana flavor that, after having swallowed the meat of the fruit, hit the back of their palates, evoking a refined retronasal pleasure.

Gazing skyward, spiraling ravens in sight, a group of coyotes are signaled to the presence of prey over two km distance from their den.

Traveling at a ground-eating trot, then bounding across the terrain, they hit destination, accosting the animals at a stiff-legged walk: head & tails held high, necks arched, nape fur erected, narrowed eyes staring — snarling, they open their mouths, exposing their teeth.

Tearing with bone-cracking jaws, they seize at necks, heads, flanks, slowing down their prey, till going in for killing bites: bodies torn open from the rear, vertebral columns undone, nasal & maxillary bones chewed away, ribs severed to open the banquet: internal organs ravaged, torn, chewed, sucked on. Predation is the strongest link in the chain of life.

Nearby, a newspaper the coyotes traipse over reads:

DR. FRANKENSTEIN'S LAIR!

In an abandoned building not far from the city, construction workers found a makeshift laboratory with shelves of human brains. The organs were meticulously arranged, categorized, and numbered, but no medical records were present. Although fresh remains were not found on site, due to the healthy bloom of the organs, investigators presumed that they were recently extracted, but no debrained corpses were about, and no nearby morgues had reported being raided. The same room contained specially prepared bones and an abundance of fleshless crania scattered across anatomy tables. While some of the skulls were intact, others had the upper parts of their craniums removed. What the brains were being used for has yet to be determined.

Discarded rumen, bits of shredded flesh, & great pieces of hide were strewn around the ungulate kill site, attracting ravens.

Descending from their hemispheres, the birds landed on the hides of the animal carcasses, poking them, ripping them, shredding them, then jumping back or up, wings out or partly extended, tails cocked.

The ravens repeated their high jumps several times, then filled their pouches and bills with fragments of suet — flying skyward, some of them dropping pieces of carrion, perhaps accidentally, perhaps in play, with bits of the remains landing on and around the newspaper.

The prevalence of bowls of rice nearby the brain room led certain factions of people to presume that the laboratory was being operated by Asians and that no more of them should be permitted to enter the country and that any and every Asian citizen should be put under investigation.

Objecting, some Asians said that the culprits could just as well be Spanish, if not more probably Brazilian.

The Spanish denied all culpability and expressed indignation over the insinuation.

Considering that the ancient Greeks saw all foreigners as barbarians, the Brazilians argued that the culprits were surely a rogue band of macabre Greek scientists and referred to them as the Gruesome Galenists.

Many Greeks objected and pointed out that Galen was from Pergamum, ergo, he was not actually Greek, but a savage Turk, at least territorially.

As the ravens cawed, the coyotes emitted high-pitched yips, followed by extended howls, sometimes culminating in a series of sharp yaps.

And the coyotes went on, sometimes barking, sometimes wailing, sometimes squealing or growling, as if in chorus with the ravens, thunderclaps provoking further howling and wailing.

Flying off in the direction of their cliff nest, taking a slanting course well above the trees, the ravens disappeared into the forest as the coyotes cached their excess kill, burying it in the earth.

One raven poked amongst the soiled & shredded bits of newspaper, which contained these illegible markings:

After further examination, it was determined that the bowls were not in fact filled with rice but human pineal glands, presumably extracted from the brains in situ.

Despite the lack of any evidence of the consumption of flesh, the scientists responsible for the macabre acts were variably being referred to as the Cartesian Cannibals, the Soul Killers, and the Third Eye Assassins, whereas others dubbed them the Hindu Maniacs.

It is unknown how many pineal glands had been extracted, or if they were equal to the number of brain specimens, but a high prevalence of them were calcified.

Soft new skeletons have been evolving beneath their shells, secreted by their epidermal layers.

The edges of the posteriors of their great upper carapaces swell, then, like surfaces suffering seismic shockwaves, their shells begin to rive, the crescive pressures of their bodies fissuring open the calcified suture lines of their exoskeletons.

Slowly withdrawing their great claws from their encasements, shedding the tendons within their muscles, their claws softening, through a progressive, scarcely perceptible effort, they extract their flesh from their shells.

With the separation of the intricate parts about the mouths and eyes, the molting reaches its final state.

Emerging from the slough, the crabs settle near their previous encasements on the sand.

Enveloped by soft, perfectly flexible skins, they sink into the loose, diaphanous mineral particles through gradual lateral motions, displacing the crystalline granules in the center beneath their bodies, progressively forcing the sand upward at their sides until the granules fall over and cover them entirely.

In time, their skin becoming as hard as thick writing paper, eventually, it amply stiffens, & they resume their natural instincts.

Exercising all their regular functions, raising themselves upright with the points of their claws, raising their pedunculated eyes as high as possible, the ganglia of their ventral nerve cords transmit signals to their organs of sense, digestion — detecting an enticing object in their vicinity, the crustaceans walk toward it, moving with celerity, darting back and forth, crawling in and out of the thing, a thick mass of matter, like a wrinkled nine pound bundle of leather crumpled over itself, a series of envelopes, folds, & ridges through which the crabs walk and burrow.

Affixing themselves to it, they grab at it, break up the surface of the object with their claws, placing bits of it in their mouths, tearing at it again and again, a vast crowd of sea creatures nourishing themselves, then lying extended in the sun, yet ever vigilant, the sound of the susurrating sea striking their statocysts.

The open cup-shaped flowers of the raspberry bush freely exposes its copious, ichorous nectar, its anthers bowing over its slender styles, its outer stamens bending away from them, releasing their pollen, their pistils swollen, their stigmas emerging, alert, sensitive, receptive. This abundant range of volumes and concentrations of nectar and pollen attracts a swarm of honeybees, who secrete the stuff from the narrow ring at the base of the receptacle, the activity of the insects increasing the size, weight, and yield of the fruit, whose scent permeates the woods, where a wolf stands, pointing its muzzle above the horizon, using a higher elevation to maximize its dynamic range, emitting a howl whose frequency changes throughout its song, its harmonic content & range of modulation fluctuating, sometimes with discontinuities in pitch.

The wolf howls for minutes, first at low frequencies, then at higher ones, the long, pure, low harmonic structure of its call sustaining its frequency before its pitch is changed, with other wolves beginning to respond, a chorus commencing, with more & more wolves joining in.

At an accelerating rate, the structure, amplitude, and pitch of their howls become shorter, higher, their frequency harmonious as the chorus continues, punctuated by squeaks, barks, growls.

As the animals get closer, the chorus grows discordant, more haphazard, their harmonics not convergent, the sound energy random, some choruses ending with barks, others with yips and yaps, as a news flash sounds over a radio, flitting through its speaker in disrupted lines, the words frequently broken by purling bursts of static:

... two more autopsied bodies ... ... in a zoo ... the heads of the victims had also been shaved, the skin of their skulls ... prompting conster....... in the com .... There is fear that a serial killer is afoot.

The lightly woody-floral blossom of the raspberries attracts the animals, who can detect even more complex synergistic relations between all the flavor metabolites of the fruit, so the animals trot off, galloping toward the clusters of raspberries, then, gathering before them, breathing in the intensity of their sweet, tangy aroma, they begin tearing away at the bushes, devouring the bounty, words concurrently flowing out of the radio in discontinuous bursts:

... surgical knife ... discovered near ... and police believe .. .. lift fingerprints ... instrument. The victims, both middle-aged, include one male and one ... It isn't known if they are related or were known to one another.

More and more wolves gather at the site, their paws bracing against the bushes, their long snouts extending outward, their noses drawn up, their lips curling back, their jaws light, fast, their peglike teeth snapping at the flesh of the berries, the fur around their mouths colored crimson as they consume the fruit in bunches, a final line surging out of the radio static:

The exacting precision of the murders makes police believe the killer is most probably a surgeon.

The wolves begin mouthing each other, seizing the heads or muzzles of their packmates, the pressure of their mouthing differing from wolf to wolf, some of them engaging in hip-thrusts as forms of communication, the acoustic spectrum of their expressive vocalizations employing the full dynamic range of their vocal chords as they squeak and whistle, exceeding the upper limits of their larynxes, the ultrasonic noises piercing through the forest, drowning out the radio transmission as they begin to whimper and whine, the harmonic sounds intensifying as they fuck, an entire pack of wolves vigorously fucking, crimson-smeared mouths opening, fangs exposed, splayed toes gripping the uneven surface of the overheated earth.

The estrogen levels of some female chimpanzees increase and peak, ripening their follicles till they rupture: — ovum released, pheromonal changes in full effect, the sight and odor of their smooth, shiny, tumescent vaginas, which protrude like immense, swollen mouths, rouses the males.

In estrus, the depth of their bulbous vaginas increase, and the males aggregate around them, but when the women repulse them, they begin foraging, knuckle-walking in loose formation across the forest floor as they eat berries and leaves, the desire for meat intensifying, biological urges exerting pressure upon their nerves, an inner, uncontrollable force taking command, possessing them, energizing their bodies.

Rummaging through the brush, one of the chimpanzees detects the scent of a Colobus monkey, prompting another to stop and examine the odor, then gaze upward toward the treetops.

Yet another touches a remnant on the ground, smells his finger, gazes into the distance, then back toward his companions, some of whom bend down to smell the remnant, then walk onward, in pursuit of the scent.

Reaching a certain locale, the carnival of chimpanzees sits in silence, waiting, watching, listening.

Mute, they scan the locale, ready to engage in a lethal territorial incursion.

At the sound of faint screeching, one of the chimps rises in silence, walks to and fro, gazing here and there, scanning the treetops again till he spots a troop of monkeys, whereby he extends his arm upward and gives out a high-pitched alarm call, hooting, screaming, announcing a raid.

Terrified, the Colobus monkeys scramble off in myriad directions.

The chimpanzees gallop wildly through the jungle, uttering louder & louder screams, running to the bases of trees, drumming on buttress roots, a percussive din erupting into a crescendo, chimps swinging from branch to branch, some scampering upward, ambling through the canopy with startling velocity, approaching their prey from a multitude of directions, as others wait below, closing in upon their target from the ground.

To counterattack, the monkeys cluster together, shrieking, leaping, biting hands, arms, scrotums, jumping on the backs of the chimps, a delirious, strident, chaotic frenzy.

Pursuing the monkeys carrying small infants, the chimps grasp them by the hands, seizing one after one of their prey, pinning them to branches, biting through the rears of their skulls and necks, conquering them, then taking their kill to the ground to consume it, fighting off hungry members of their party.

Bereft of flesh, one chimp fingers an object on the ground. Gazing at it in bewilderment, lifting it up in the air, unsure which direction to hold it in, examining it, turning it, unfolding its parts, a series of thin serrated pages containing markings foreign to its consciousness.

Detectives noted that, after further investigation, they discovered anthropometers, boley gauges, spreading calipers, and other anthropological tools at the laboratory, in addition to a sign which read, "Man still bears in his bodily frame the indelible stamp of his lowly origin." It's now believed that the suspects are not surgeons, but most probably a group of psychopathic anthropologists.

Several of the chimps, their bodies riddled with puncture wounds, devour the carcasses of what they have caught, drawing and quartering them, chewing on limbs, savoring muscle tissue, brains, bone, hair, viscera.

The noise of bones cracked and crunched and the ripping of skin resonate throughout the jungle.

While other chimps approach them, stretching out their hands, thrusting upturned palms in their faces, gently placing their fingertips near to or even inside the lips of the hunters, they turn away, rebuking their rivals in open sight of the community, giving morsels only to abiding allies.

Continuing to play with the paper, the chimp folds it into different configurations, seeming in fact to be reading the object, prompting other chimps to laugh.

They also found shovels, trowels, knives, sticks, stones, and branches, as well as an array of nut casings, bits of broken shells, & nut fragments, some of which may contain identifying teeth marks.

When drops of blood and bone fragments fall from the canopy above, the remnants of a meal another chimp is devouring from on high, the younger baby chimps clamber to the spoils, seizing the excess.

Hoping for food, a few females approach the hunters, walking backwards toward them, presenting their asses to the males, attempting to entice them with their distended, shimmering vaginas.

As the male chimps gaze back & forth, looking at the meat, looking at the women, then back at the meat, deliberating whether to continue eating, or to fuck, the female chimps rear directly onto their erect cocks, prompting the male chimps to pause eating to fuck, carcasses clutched as they ensue, the females stretching their hands behind them to take food from the mouths of the males, or directly snatch at the meat dangling from their hands.

In the midst of this ribaldry, the rebuked chimps approach the one with the newspaper and clutch at it, tearing it to pieces, leaving only fragments of text behind:

Notes on the size ... neocortex ... expansion ... comparative analyses ... red ... claw ...

As they migrate into Africa from Spain, between astronomical twilight and dawn, an eerie supersonic frequency compels a flock of European Pied Flycatchers to stop their frequent zigzagging movements to approach the sound, to slow down before the entity emitting it, and, in stillness, to observe it.

Although its movement is highly accelerated, imperceptible to human sense organs, it is visible to the birds, whose critical clicker fusion frequency, operating at 120 frames per second, enables them to have a vastly detailed view of the phenomenon, its shifting motions and mutating forms mesmerizing them.

In its midst, in a state of captivation, the birds began singing a series of figures, each separated by a strong cæsura, creating a complex array of strophes, recombining their varying figures in a seeming endless catena of unique ways. Unlike blues or pop song formats, the Pied Flycatchers create a highly varied repertoire of song types, ranging from A B A B C D C D C D to A B A B A B A B A B C D C C & then to the even more complex A B A B A B C D E F G H F G H and beyond, with some of their compositions exceeding 100 different figures, as if each were created to correspond to the shifting mutations of the strange entity, as if composing not by instinct, but spontaneously.

She awoke on an autopsy table; felt a thick needle slowly exiting her skin.

Drowsy, she saw nothing but a dark, indeterminate shape standing over her, the figure a mere blurry image she could not bring into focus.

As the doctor gazed into her eyes, a thought emerged in her, one distinct from her own —— a totally foreign, strange, disquieting thought.

It entered her like an alien object manifesting at the nerve level. It was a sensation and form of cogitation not her own. It felt as if something else was suddenly breathing inside of her, as if her blood were pulsing differently, as if the core of her body was being penetrated from deep within.

If she seemed to understand this thought in a roughly primordial way — no, it was more of an intestinal or gastric sensation, as if a sanguine humoral force was enveloping her —, she could not decipher it with her mind, just as she could not focus her eyes to perceive the image imprinted on her retina, as if her eyes were failing, or refusing, to perceive what they were perceiving, or as if scratches in her cornea produced distorted images, like cracked camera lenses fracturing all incoming light, the matter leaving only distorted impressions on the film emulsion.

Despite her struggle to speak, to articulate something that she was not thinking but which was being thought within her, projected into her, silently, as if under the hand of a ventriloquist, she could not transform it into words.

Although she did not hear any words per se, it was as if a language, or rather, some perplexing form of communication entirely foreign to her, was being sounded inside of her and she struggled to grasp it without knowing its words or coding.

In the room, an African Grey was speaking, or imitating human speech, pronouncing the words "man is the only talking animal, the only talking animal."

Gazing at the doctor half in astonishment, half in fright, she tried to speak again, as if the thought inside of her was her own, but it was like trying to engage in a form of intercourse she was incapable of, a language her tongue lacked the facility for, as if suddenly attempting to perform a high wire act when one had never trained as an acrobat, when one's limbs had never practiced such movements, did not know how to execute them, could not execute them, and when she stepped out onto the rope, she plummeted into an abyss. — It was as if she was trying to speak hieroglyphically, and her tongue dammed up, twisted, trembled in her mouth, beat spasmodically against her palate, rocked back and forth against her molars as if her body was attempting to perform an action it could never achieve, an action that required an entirely other physiology, genetic composition, motor function.

A flash of clarity rendered her to a pulp.

Did she see what she thought she saw, or was it an illusory distortion? The effects of anesthesia, or some other drug? A hallucination, or some phantom or imaginary experience?

As she thrust her arms outward toward the doctor, to combat him, to refuse the communication, a violent electrical charge shot through her nervous system, the intensity of which rendered her unconscious.

The parrot continued sounding off, shuttling back and forth across its perch, uttering soft, subtle noises that resembled laughter.

Moving beyond the stasis of quotidian time into the eonic, beyond anthropomorphic sight into cosmic perception, into geological temporality, where rock and mountain are not fixed forms or entities, but great assemblages of matter in continuous development, matter that is moving, in constant variation and flux — every milieu is vibratory: collisional mountain belts, immense pieces of continental crust, collide, with neither plate subducting, for both are buoyant granitic masses that crumple and rise: buckling, warping, deforming geological structures of bordering territories, folding sedimentary and igneous rock into dense, crystalline metamorphic rock. Matter put into extreme strain by compressional tectonic forces & high-pressure conditions; minerals from the surface of the earth exposed to high-pressure forges, forcing them to recrystallize into a multitude of novel forms;

crustal blocks condensing one against another; geological pressures deep within the core of mountain ranges intensifying, forming fiercely compacted, high-grade metamorphic matter wherein violent tensional forces enfold sediments & minerals into new shapes: feldspar, clay, and other layered sediment are pressed into mica, biotite, muscovite, staurolite, and calcareous, psammitic, & matic schist. What seems hard, fixed, but unchangeable granite stratum, was twisted, folded, molded anew by slow, grinding forces bending it into entirely different shapes — every apparently inert mass is a whorl of moving atoms: not bound form, not permanent, settled matter, rather, a dance of forces, densities, iridescent chaos, like magnetic fields spontaneously created by the thermal battery effects in every rotating body — superseding the fragile environments required by biological forms, magnetic ones arise even in the serene thermal degradation of cosmic territorialities. Convection & turbulence produce cyclonic properties and thereby generate magnetic fields that are amplified and rise to the surface: density reductions become extreme, internal stresses dominate, birthing non-equilibrium and rapid reconnection, dissipation, escape, and expansion, magnetic flux generated in stars, in galaxies, a host of thermal and magnetic forces rendering nonvisual forces visible, as wind, carrying seeds from neighboring limestone mountains, spurs germination, yet a paucity of limestone retards the development, with luxuriantly flourishing siliceous species overtaking and subjugating the seeds, dead plant residues decomposing, forming humus, brown and black mass, divergent and contrasting vegetation, plants settling on the bare earth with a substratum wholly devoid of humus .... slowly, they conquer even the most barren of rock, the barest boulders, & what is ostensibly most inert, shifting sands: lichens, mosses, crucifers, saxifrages & so on, their spores, seeds, & fruits set forth on lines of flight, carried by winds, a milieu of materials in nomadic transference from domain to domain, making incursions into the sharpest slopes and the most adamant crags. — All is there in mountains, as centuries of cultural colors and refractions live on within the geological terrain of homo sapiens, layered like ordered strata superimposed on one another, but also dislocated, replete with fault lines, hidden in its seas, forests, plants, and mountains, the entire continuum of the past continuing to flow through the species in a multitude of conduits, as sputtering through a cloud of static, a news report flows in medias res over a radio: ... *the phrase "I care for nothing, all shall go sealed within the iron hills," which, although highly cryptic, detectives revealed to be the first major clue to the surgical crimes, evidence of a nihilistic sociopath. At this point in time, what specific hills the murderer is referring to is not known, but it is probable that other bodies are contained there. While police have not yet released images of the murderer's notebook, they stated that it contained another terrifying line, "they must nevertheless eventually perish," indicating the murderer's insatiable drive to kill yet more and more people. How many, who knows. The passage they said was written in a halting, nearly illegible script, seemingly frantically scribbled out, as if a flashing thought to be captured before erasure, or as if written in a highly agitated state, signs perhaps of psychotic derangement. An apparent motive has still not been discerned.*

The bonobos use of lexigrams had become more and more complex, with the animals employing them in a wide variety of contexts, in the absence of referents, & spontaneously, communicating with each other with the lexigrams on their own, separate from humans, not prompted by commands, requests, or as part of controlled experiments, often sitting before their lexigram keyboards to compose extended thoughts, including entire paragraphs, which they sometimes printed and read to themselves.

A number of the animals even began playing with writing instruments & learned to hold pens and to form letters and words and to write basic sentences, their linguistic abilities extending to giving individuals proper names, denoting common objects, identifying actions, locations, and properties, moving beyond merely effective procedures for fulfilling desires to comprehending psychologically referential communication & learning to inform others of things to, in a sense, presenting 'news' of events, as if, somehow, they were beginning to enter history, to document their existence, to express a newly born reflective consciousness, a consciousness amplified by their interaction with signifiers.

After playing water-chase and tickling his confreres, one of the bonobos went to retrieve some bananas, grapes, and peanuts from inside the lab.

As he was peeling a banana, he gazed at the desk of one of the researchers and, concealed amongst her papers, he noticed a lexigram letter that one of the other bonobos had secreted there, its legible parts startling him.

Dropping the banana, the primate sat in the chair before the desk and, upon reading the entirety of the report, grew increasingly furious, his face flushing with astonishment and rage.

Despite the letter not being signed, from its phrasing & style of thinking, he could determine the identity of the author.

Incensed, he gazed about the room, hooting, yelping, grunting and, in a state of vehemence, began tearing up all of the papers on the desk and overturning and smashing objects in the room.

As if in imitation of a human, he stood as erect as possible, his jaw receding, his sloped vocal tract bending in the process, his tongue lowering a bit down, thereby shortening the distance between his soft palate and the back of his throat.

With his nasal passage partially blocked off, turbulent microbursts of air began to flow through his mouth with great rapidity as he began making sounds which at times seemed like consonants, with him uttering more and more noises, each apparently a command, the consonants breaking into long extended vowels, till more and more consonants and vowels came together, an ever more intricate and nuanced chain of letters and syllables, making it sound as if he was forming words, with the other bonobos screaming *wraaah wraaah wraaah* in response, uttering soft barks at the writer, stretching their arms, frantically shaking their hands in the air, them too full of terrifying fury.

Although she tried to flee, the writer was swiftly surrounded and the other bonobos began directing aimed kicks at her with their feet and barking, the pitch of their calls intensifying, them screaming, the timbre of their vowel sounds brightening as they attacked her with vigor, their bodies tense, rigid, the kicks more violent, more forceful, more powerful, them thrashing her with greater and greater intensity, then bashing her skull in and tearing her body to pieces.

Amidst the debris of smashed objects, bits of bonobo carcass, skull pieces, torn papers, and battered fruit were remnants of the lexigram letter: *dig, hurt, look, come, hide, surprise, bad, monster, broken, knife, secret, fight, goodbye, puzzle, red, humans, look*, all of which provoked the troop of bonobos to enact further violence, whereby, with vigorous primal force, they began destroying the lab, demolishing everything within it, rendering to pieces what they could, smashing objects, shattering windows, pulverizing walls, finally somehow setting the building aflame, then fleeing into the streets as the blaze began to take hold, spread, and flicker in the sky, a proliferation of wildly colored tongues of fire, burning, blazing, glowing, the first conflagration ever instigated by animals.

For eons, they did not exist, at least not on earth, & then, slowly, gradually, they came to be, emerging through a long struggle, through various genetic lines, evolving over time, through different mutations, being themselves a kind of mutation, eventually somehow breaking from the chain, separating from and entirely forgetting their cousins, seeing them not in fact as guests, but as the most alien of strangers, yet the increase began moderately, sensibly, soundly, with a population of circa 170 million homo sapiens in Year 1 of the Common Era expanding to circa 300 million over the duration of a long eight centuries, and so, still, there was room to breathe, and the earth was plentiful and nature was abundant & the jungle remained a heart of darkness,

and with the population expanding to only circa 500 million by the late 16th century, still, even in this near tripling of the number of human inhabitants of the earth since Year 1, there was room to breathe, there was air, there was light, there was space, for the velocity of life was commensurate with the velocity of the technology of the rising speck of dust, but, increasingly, the animal kingdom felt the encroaching presence of those other strange creatures, the likes of which they had never before encountered,

and with the population expanding to circa 750 million by the mid 18th century, still, in the face of the multitude of its surging edifices, expanding as it did horizontally and vertically, there was more than enough room to breathe, for the candle, the horse, and the telescope continued to rule, and the velocity of life was sensible, trotting forward with the rhythm of the Equidæ family, with the population expanding to circa 1 billion by the 1800s, just as zoos were beginning to be established and monkeys were making a name for themselves, taking a long 17 centuries to nearly quadruple since Year 1, hence, still, even at this late point in what those creatures called *civilization*, even with the advent of rail travel and steam locomotion, there was room to breathe, for electricity had not yet crackled through the cities, though germ theory was in sight, but the vigorous little speck of dust hadn't surged outward too much,

yet, with the population inflating to circa 1.5 billion in the late 19th century, as the pace of everything began to rapidly increase with the swift transmission of telegraph messages (commencing with the ominous phrase, "*What hath God wrought?*"...) and the birth of the car, still, there was room to breathe, but industrialization was escalating extinction rates and, like a tidal wave overflowing multitudes of boundaries, or like a lunatic running amok in a menagerie, speed was taking over and anonymity was usurping individuality, but, after the murder of paganism, no sodomic ethic was in place — having long ago given themselves a metaphysical command, including a metaphysical command against sodomy *&* onanism, *be fruitful, they said, & multiply, without reserve, exponentially* → → →

and so, despite germ warfare, & with the birth of the supermarket and the strip mall and the airplane, in the age of radio waves & antibiotics, the number of homo sapiens doubled from 1 billion to circa 2 billion by the early 20th century, the entire world population of 1804 exuded from uteri like radiation from the sun in merely 120 years yet, if, still, there was sufficient room to breathe, it was fast decreasing, with evodeviation distorting ecological relationships and reducing the capacity of ecosystems to support health & life, but despite its phylogenetic maladjustment, or because of it, the human animal could not control its itch to procreate, and it did not propagate in relation to its arable land, nor did it do so with the sagacity of a tribe, nor did it fuck like an animal, for it was more and more removed from its terrain and it was less and less erotic and the hunter gave way to the shopper and that consumer rarely ever thought of the future, rarely too did it think epochally or eonically, but mostly of social status and of pensions, of eternal convenience and comfort, never of the planet's edge, never of finitude, hardly of death, though, as no other species, it preserved its dead, saving them for eternity, leaving yet less & less room for other species,

and with the population swelling to circa 2.5 billion by the mid 20th century, if, still, there happened to be some room to breathe, there was yet less and less of it, just as there was less and less darkness, though more and more of it, for, with unremitting deforestation and unremitting breeding, — the two go hand in hand, like space in time, like hominid in human, — oxygen is consumed faster than it is replaced, for half of the tropical forests on the planet had been severely damaged or entirely destroyed, but in the age of space travel and of planetary expansion, the human species was blasting forward with the pulsionary zing of a rocket, its florescence concomitant with the decay in habitat and the disintegration of species richness and composition, for life lives on death and the human soul is the most potent of poisons,

and so, by the Millennium of the Common Era, when the world population had doubled in a swift 30 plus years to circa 6.2 billion, almost as instantaneously as an email could circle the globe, since, *still*, no sodomic ethic was in place *&* immediacy and impulse ruled, the itch to procreate spread as fast as an infectious disease, as if it were an irrepressible addiction, disseminated as wantonly as light traveling through the universe, uteri naturally and artificially inseminated (*more options, more options — get the turkey baster! cloning, cloning, let's replicate ourselves said the bastards*), bursting like geysers, making for an increase of over 3600% of the population since Year 1 of the Common Era, with homo sapiens splitting from the womb faster than the number of blinks it could make per second, with the velocity and haste of text messages, an increase biologists refer to as swarming, the boom-and-bust pattern followed by plagues of mice, swarms of locusts, and weevils in flour, and so, in the face of scurvy, beriberi, typhoid, cholera, smallpox, influenza, coronary disease and cancer, and *as* forms of scurvy, beriberi, typhoid, cholera, smallpox, influenza, coronary disease and cancer, the species proliferated as it extended itself even into distant space, and there was less & less room to breathe, less & less nature, more and more carbon dioxide, less & less animals, less & less insects, more and more light, less & less flowering plants, less & less arable land, less & less light and more and more darkness, yet still not enough anal and oral sex, just less, less, & less, but not the lessness of the wise,

and in the face of climatological catastrophes, in the face of force multipliers exacerbating world health problems, still, the population exploded to over 8 billion, and with circa 5 births per second, 16,000 per hour, 400,000 per day, 140+ million per year, nearly the total world population of the 2nd century was born anew annually, *an entire earthful of people in just 365 days*, an ocean of placentas &

vaginal muck ending in an average of one homo sapiens per every 7500 m² of habitable though not arable land, ending in less & less oxygen per person, less & less space, and less & less grain, with the bipedal species and their domesticated animals making up 96% of the mass of mammals on the planet, equal that is to the total mass of dark energy and dark matter in the universe (*the only place where darkness remains*), with only 4% being everything else, from elephants to badgers to tigers and bats, with humanity weighing six times as much as all wild mammals, ergo, with radical declines in biodiversity, declines nearly as indiscriminate as tidal waves, for everything is faster in the insta-epoch, with *still* no sodomic ethic in place, and with less and less relation with the natural world, the ecosystem is perverted as indiscriminately as a tweet is dispatched, and the transmission of the infectious diseases of humans, other animals, and plants increases with hypersonic rapidity, for this is the age of the hypersonic and everything happens at terrifying velocities, velocities beyond regular sense perception, velocities that rupture organs, velocities that blind the species, for little is visible at the speed of myopia,

and so, with less and less natural terrain left on earth, and with the domains of animals undergoing precipitous to near total erasure, as the paratenic host invades every locale in its purview, penetrating even to the depths of the oceans, more and more animals and insects began to inhabit certain human provinces, with animals taking up residence in graveyards and churches, for those were the emptiest of spaces, with graveyards being one of the last places left on earth with any remnant of nature, & the only space entirely devoid of homo sapiens, that is, live ones, animals and insects began to people there, displacing gravestone markers, displacing graves, inhabiting mausoleums, disinterring bodies in the process, making fertile earth of decaying carcasses, nesting and playing, till those burial sites became more like jungles, mountains, and forests, the sole places where there was light, air, and space, the sole places where there was room to breathe, where there were no hieratic edifices or economic palaces, just open terrain in which animals could roam free of the presence of that uncanny species which, in dreadful fear of death, guarded and stored up its dead,

and so, when members of the species went to pay respects to their kith & kin, horror gave way to fear, and, like the first humans entering the jungle, they grew terrified, for their graveyards had been overtaken and they were becoming like new hearts of darkness, terra incognitæ they were reluctant to enter, where light did not permeate, where neon signs were absent, where digital displays did not exist, and slowly, the names and dates on the headstones grew illegible with each brushing of animal skin and insect wing against stone, with each establishment of a nest or resting place: consonants effaced, inadvertently sanded to nothing by bristly hides, nails, teeth, piss, shit, and semen, vowels eventually effaced too, till no more words were visible, till dates too had been effaced, the headstones losing their sculpted and chiseled elements, their edges worn away, the hand of man eradicated, making the markers of life and death indistinguishable, the headstones no longer headstones, only stones, once again purely granite, marble, or slate, as if, in the face of its construction of contrived bulwarks against the dire forces of nature, mankind's seemingly permanent but fragile fortresses in the air, the animals and insects were, although apparently mute, although apparently devoid of speech, profoundly expressive, profoundly conscious, profoundly insightful, enacting on a subtle physical scale the entropic forces of nature, a thermodynamic law that, despite the most ingenious technological inventions, could not be combatted, that, despite its grandest efforts, despite its attempts at preserving itself for eternity, despite its attempts to outwit death, from spirituality to cryonics, it is always defeated, nature dismantles its bulwarks with ease, splintering them like cracking spaghetti, whether through volcanic, seismic, tidal, or microscopic means, from explosions to spirochetes, every human endeavor, from the work of the Sumerians to the work of Silicon Valley, is sundered, turned to dust, obliterated as if it were but vapor, mere rock to be pulverized, like matter in black holes, nothing escaping but annihilated, from the pyramids of Giza to espresso machines, from the Lydians to the Aztecs, from museums to the mind's precincts of memory, all will be made manure, cosmic dust, innominate debris, for death comes not to individuals alone, but to entire species as well, rendering the daring adventure of reason powerless before the sublime forces of the cosmos, putting all metaphysics on ice, not as an act of preservation, not as a cryonic gesture enacted to overcome death, but to make metaphysics of every form suffer exposure to harsh elements, to make it freeze to death in the thermal chill of space — nature is not cryonic, it is thermodynamic,

and in their muteness, the animals and insects were playing out that law to demonstrate with expressive force to mankind, that most spiritual of animals, that most unnatural of animals, those clowns who endowed even history with spirit, that cryonic buffoon par excellence, that it too could never escape the indifferent grinding deathmill of the cosmos, that it too, as all its works, from the most banal to the most magisterial, would crack apart like a dehiscent seed & burst into pieces & disintegrate, rocks for worms to crawl through, nothing but a shoreline of anonymous particles . . . .

   and it was then that a radio emission sounded in the air, sputtering through bursts of static like a series of interrupted telegraph messages, reporting on *the destruction of religious artifacts throughout the world, that in libraries, museums, & elsewhere, ritual Judaic, Christian, and Islamic objects, from rosaries to phylacteries, prayer rugs, & books, had been burned, smeared with excrement, torn to pieces, or stolen, with one report stating that a mixture of objects from different religions had been set upon a chessboard, while animals and insects of all kinds, from birds to dragonflies to monkeys to pigs, were witnessed in stoups and ghusl buildings, while another report stated that, in script replicating each of the different scribes, the multiple portions of the Codex Sinaiticus each contained an exegesis declaring that, in the beginning was the* lokhos, not the logos, *you misheard, for the lower mouth speaks before the higher.*

In many regions of the world, dust storms erupted, with howling winds carrying loose soil into the air, blackening skies, obscuring the sun, darkening windows, cloistering much of the population. Although it persisted for weeks, the meteorological crisis was incomparable to the new pandemic, the effects of which were intensified by continuing dust storms, tornadoes, and hurricanes, all of which ærosolized microbes, with debris and waste harboring fecal coliforms and enteropathogens, and water, air, and vector-borne pathogens giving birth to vibrio vulnificus and other bacterial diseases. Some likened the event to a biblical apocalypse, others to a human one, the inevitable effusions of a havoc-wreaking species gone berserk, and yet others to a natural disaster, which was perhaps no different. With death tolls exceeding the tens of millions, school systems and businesses all closed in an attempt to regulate and control the further spread of pathogens. Strict shelter-in-place commands having been issued by government leaders from country to country around the world, nearly all social activity ceased, for the sheer terror before transmitted bacterium, fungal toxins, and viral diseases like glanders and anthrax petrified most of the population. Who wanted pus-filled ulcerations, or necrotic fasciitis?

Public and private transport having come to a full stop at sea and on land and in air, the global AQI fell from 300+ to below 25, resulting in an ambient air concentration not known since the early

1800s. After days, the near-total absence of the presence of the human species opened the earth to the animal kingdom, to its reterritorialization, with a greater and greater number of animals & insects inhabiting what were principally solely human domains. The ending of the extreme meteorological events coupled with the cessation of the frenetic activity of the upright species resulted in a measurable absence of noise and the onset of a quietude hitherto unknown on the planet. With the muting of the technological din, the tumultuous music of nature pervaded the planet, & even urban centers sounded like jungles due to the wild proliferation of animals in its streets, trees, and public squares.

As the dangers of the pandemic persisted, with new, more pervasive outbreaks resulting from the flouting of shelter-in-place guidelines, health organizations around the world issued draconian rules of law. For months, social activities remained forbidden, ergo, ants, bees, wasps and other insects abounded as never before, their numbers in fact swiftly increasing, with some near-extinct species beginning to increase & flourish anew. Outbreaks from zoos led to wolves, leopards, and other large animals emerging in suburban locales, including gorillas & monkeys, who ambled into delis, supermarkets, and sometimes churches, synagogues, or mosques, for they contained many objects from which the primates could swing or play upon. The monkeys reveled in the sound of their screeching and laughter echoing in the empty spiritual buildings in which they frolicked.

The extreme isolation & extended forced self-enclosing was vexing to most of the populace, whose nerves frayed, were lacerated as if by nettles, or an amalgam of abiotic and psychological pressures. Psyches strained, emotions tested, all sense of reality dimming, states of paranoia or delirium were provoked by the fear of death. When passing before mirrors, they did not see themselves, but flashes of fronds, anaerobic bacteria, or violent swirls of microbes. Staring more directly into the looking glass, the images that returned were blurry, distortions, unclear or grotesque projections, or so they supposed: swimming protoplasm, double-ventricle hearts, pointed ears, gilled & tailed embryos, lanugic bodies. When gazing with great intensity into the silvered glass, as if trying to focus the returning image through sheer will, fragments of pictures would emerge and disappear: indiscriminate amalgamations of themselves with fish, amphibians, reptiles, mammals.

Rubbing their eyes, the members of the species gazed again, struggling to form pictures of only themselves. Often, the reflections looked more like dada collages. At times, some people thought they saw images of hominids, or unsettling pliocenic visions, as if mirrors were becoming phantasmagoric prisms, fun house mechanisms, or screens upon which were projected the delirious films of the primal unconscious exploding forth like terrifying mescaline chimeras made flesh.

When confronted with intermittent images of chimpanzees, people thought they must have been suffering from inebriating fevers, or that the increasing presence of animals made them see, or think they were seeing, animals everywhere. Was this collective mass hysteria? A series of planet-wide hallucinations? Protein deficiency deliria? Perhaps a pathogen from the pandemic had infected them — did they believe that walls could safeguard them from bacteria, that such would not seep through some crack in the façade, that their bodies were firmer than rock? Did they forget that minerals themselves are porous and full of perforations?

After quickly turning from their mirrors and suddenly sensing an animal in their midst, they wondered if it was an apparition, a natural psychedelic event, or the visual aftereffect of having stared into a mirror for too long, of a too long isolation, of disorientation from severe weather and other perilous social & global conditions, or the actual intrusion of an animal in their private domain, which was altogether possible. Reality itself seemed to have become a hall of carnival mirrors, but then, any sense of what reality was had become increasingly tenuous and, in isolation, what was dream, fantasy, hallucination? What reality? Did each not begin to intersect and fuse, with none therefore being distinguishable? And in isolation, what were they themselves? Did their humanity, or their perception of it, somehow begin to dissipate? Did it exist beyond perception? What was the human, some few repeated to themselves? Was it not the laughing animal? The toolmaker? The rational animal? Is not language what separates man from beast, what makes the quintessence of dust the paragon of animals? Are we not, they repeated, the crown of all creation? Or is all being only what is perceived, with you becoming an animal if you perceive that you are one? *Esse est percipi*...

The optical machine of the mirror did not however relent and, having become unreliable, an object that no longer obeyed natural law but functioned as if subatomic reality *&* reality had been inverted, many shrouded it in fabric, or smashed it to pieces in moments of fury or terror, as if the object itself gave rise to the phenomenon. Ultimately, the obscuring or destruction of it was immaterial, for the mind itself became an optical machine *&* projections, like holograms of the eye, phosphenic specters, or species-pervasive mirages, manifested without relent. Nothing seemed continuous any longer, but quantized, reality itself a severe radical intangibility, as if the very atoms of which it is comprised were continuously cracking into pieces at the speed of light, with particles never localizing, always in multiple places, always disintegrating and reconfiguring with such velocity that nothing could be discerned with particularity — nothing was independent, unitary, fixed, stable, or whole; rather, all became but continuous chaos, a constant dynamic interaction between the body and other living organisms, resulting in frequent suicides, madness, or prolonged states of sleep or catatonia, as if the entire earth were a space station and the population had been put into states of suspended animation to prepare it for a journey elsewhere.

When the pandemic subsided, although fear & terror eventually gave way, remnants of both remained, erupting like traumatic flashbacks, or unwelcome and debilitating spasms, and as the species slowly returned to its public spaces, insects and animals began to retreat or flee to their usual domains. Yet, it took months to empty libraries, museums, synagogues, churches, and mosques of the invaders that had colonized them, just as it took months to clean up the aftermath of debris, which now also included remnants of insects and animals and their nests & habits: eggshells, feces, dead embryos, bones of prey, feathers, and the like. The religious buildings in particular were insectuous, had throughout the duration of the pandemic become insectan orders, no longer spiritual houses, but the habitats of hexapod invertebrates, where theology had no place, only entomology. *In the beginning was the worm*, not the word.

At first, the density of the inhabitants made it all but impossible to enter them. When crossing the threshold of the insecta, pandemonium erupted, for the buildings had become thickets of bugs, with insects seething in every direction, ricocheting off the bodies of whoever entered, latching onto them, clinging to limbs, entwining themselves in people's hair, creeping underneath their clothing, entering every open orifice, from mouths to nostrils to ears, crawling and slithering into anuses, cocks, vaginas, assailing eyes & lips, engulfing whoever crossed their domain, riddling them with abysmal fright, provoking more interpretations of coming apocalypses, the Final Judgment, or Yawm ad-Din, whereas rabbis knew that conquest and settlement does not occur quickly, but slowly and gradually. The churches were surprisingly bright too, as luminous as never before, since the colors in all the stained glass windows had somehow gone clear, resulting in the bright, illuminating light of the sun at last penetrating those gloomy precincts.

With patience, the spiritual buildings were eventually emptied of their unwelcome inhabitants, though many remained, appearing every now and then in the midst of the rare and infrequent sermons, descending from vaulted ceilings like miniature comets, causing many people to flee while others remained *&* welcomed the descent of the bugs, likening the attacks to adorning themselves with living cilices. Locust *&* other insect shell remnants were regularly found crushed between pages of the Talmud, the Bible, and the Qur'ān, while hornets' nests adhered to Torah arks like octopuses, encrusted themselves around crosses like barnacles, and clung onto minarets like leeches. Thinking of Exodus 23, the priests decided to leave the nests as portents and signals, not of an ensuing apocalypse, but of the presence of the deity, of its literal manifestation *&* the fulfillment of "the word of God."

When the hornets' nests fell from the crosses or were torn apart by animals searching for larvæ, the crucifixes were at last cleaned, astonishing the priests, who discovered that, in church after church around the world, each Christ had been carved or sculpted anew to resemble an ape. An outcry erupted over what the Vatican deemed acts of coordinated global vandalism, crimes that they believed had to have been organized by a conspiracy of evolutionists, atheists, or anarchist artists, if not animal activists, and many of each faction claimed to be the culprits behind the gesture. Alternatively, thinking of the Hadith wherein Abu Hurrairah quoted the prophet Mohammed's statement that Jesus will come & break the cross, kill the pigs, and abolish the Jizya, some Imams interpreted the event as Allah's destruction of every religion & sect other than Islam and, to ratify their viewpoint, looked for children playing with snakes. Another faction of imams thought it a symbolic mystical event signifying Allah's transformation of transgressors into apes & pigs, despite the lack of any swine imagery, or human-swine hybrids, though the multitude of many pig-like humans gave rise to doubt. If many humans looked contemptuously upon pigs, a human-like pig would be a far worse creature. Talmudic scholars remained mute on the event since they could not cease arguing between themselves over literal versus figurative senses of it, affirming and refuting each interpretation, with some accusing others of engaging in *eisegesis* and not *exegesis*, while still others both adopted and contested the figurative sense, thereby refusing to ever come to a definitive conclusion, which was prototypically Talmudic of them. Despite the fact that apiarists deal with bees, not hornets, hordes of evangelicals denounced them, decrying them to be the evil villains behind the ape-Christs. In vengeance, they smashed honey jars everywhere and committed acts of arson, burning down honey factories throughout the country, which, although it did not restore the Christ, or lead to a mystic reversal of the crucifixes, did attract hordes of bears, but not vegans. To entomologists, the pervasive presence of insects and animals was indicative of an imbalance in the ecosystem and they doubted whether symbiosis and trans-species interdependence would ever emerge. When the hornets' nests were collected as potential evidence, after they were warmed up, some remaining hornets emerged from them, stinging everyone in their midst.

Their sensilla hit with a frenzy of vibrations, an immense cloud of Calliphoridæ ceased their frantic, zigzagging flight patterns & coordinated their legs, wings, and halteres, rotating about their axes of yaw & pitch, swirling in place before a mutating entity that had startled them into near stillness.

The Calliphoridæ were hovering before something whose velocity was so fleet it exceeded human perception. To a woman standing nearby, its details were obscure, appearing to be nothing but a dark, shifting, indistinct, blurry mass, like something from the distant past shooting through space like an arrow of time, millions of years or more unfolding in a blinding flash.

In contrast, in their vibrating immobility, the Calliphoridæ resembled a colossal bright metallic blue-black and silver period, a pulsating circle of charged particles marking the sky as if a buzzing concrete poem. The sheer density of the cloud of bugs, which in their intimate movement became a single enormous object, turned the cluster of their bright metallic silver-blue abdomens into a reflecting shield that scintillated in the sun.

Seized by this play of dark iridescent vittæ, the woman began filming it, her eyes perceiving but 60 discrete flashes of light per second, whereas the Calliphoridæ perceived 250, their rhabdomeres consisting of stacks of ~30,000–50,000 microvilli each, photoreceptors that made the world something else entirely for them, their vision being infinitely sharper and faster. Where the human saw only steady light, or seemingly steady objects & believed its reality was reality itself, the Calliphoridæ saw what was what, getting closer to the real, closer to the velocity of matter, closer to the uncanny phenomenon unfolding before them.

The energetic force of the blurry mass was so powerful that the Calliphoridæ continued to hover before it, almost as if it impeded their forward movement, the sonic terror of their flagellar vibrations hitting nearly 300 Hz and mounting.

As if reacting to a surging geothermal or volcanic force, with the increasing speed of the air current, the steady deviation and restoring torque of the joints of the Calliphoridæ increased, the resonance frequency of their wings rising even higher as the condensed block of insects burst apart into a chaotic spray.

When they dispersed into innumerable directions at 1.5 meters per second, the woman turned toward the indistinct blurry mass and filmed it zooming over the terrain like a photon bolting from a laser.

When the employees entered the library following the aftermath of the pandemic, they encountered a confused environment where animal, human, and other domains intersected, blending to such a degree that each troubled the precise definition or nature of the other. The sound of strange, distorted, if not terrifying voices, like drunk or deranged people, coupled with the hurried noise of fleeing, of doors banging with great force and windows slammed open, made them wonder if homeless people or asylum inmates had inhabited the building. Was it then any longer a library, or was it some amalgam of places? How had the site, as many others, undergone transformation & mutation in the midst of all the world cataclysms? What *word* cataclysms, what categorical designations that is, did the world cataclysms spawn? The "Public" having been nearly erased, the name on the building, whatever it had become, only read *u   rar*

Although the space was relatively intact, with its books and other materials mostly being in place, & although it suffered no serious structural damage, the library was overrun with nature, lianas having penetrated its interior, snaking along walls & ceilings, cracking through surfaces, effacing the distinction between internal & external. Through shattered windows and open doors, wind had brought dust, soil, leaves, and other natural and human debris, turning the carpets and tiles into forest floors, replete with rotting wood, leaf and plant litter, invertebrates, fungi, archæa and similar forest elements. More startling yet was the presence of numerous large and small animals, from donkeys and hyenas to monkeys, parrots, and kookaburras, whose noises resounded throughout the space, making for a wild, frequently hysterical racket. With no patrons, and despite the presence of books, the library had become a jungle, if not circus, and it had the distinct odor of both.

As the employees wandered about, they also came upon mirrors that had not previously been in the library, and myriad other strange objects, including a multitude of glass jars of what resembled embryos preserved in formaldehyde. Whether human, animal, or gaffes, was not certain, for each looked eerily similar, almost indistinguishable from one another, but they were carefully staged, placed as if a scientific display & surrounded with images of seeds, stars, stones, geological strata, & maps of the cosmos. Though lacking taxonomic specifications, or any scientific nomenclature, the comic style of the lettering on the nameplates below the glass jars, *Human? Animal? Monster?!* and the presence nearby of posters of Marie-Angelique LeBlanc, the Wild Boy of Hanover, the Nocturnal Man, *Homo Sylvestris, Homo Ferus*, and *Homo Monstrosus* made the presentation less of a natural history one and more of a freak show attraction or 19th century medical exhibit.

When walking by the mirrors, the employees caught glances of other animals, thought, more specifically, that they were seeing apes. Affrighted, they rapidly turned about, but nothing was there, save themselves.

Was it the still lingering presence of animals that made them think they were seeing things that weren't actually present, certainly not right next to them? Was it the effects of a fever, a symptom of the new virus? Were they phantom images or formed hallucinations? Or were they merely detecting ape-like features in themselves and imagining that they were seeing apes, unconsciously extending something ancient and archaic in their genetic makeup, provoked by the altered character of the space, complex afterimages made up of the visual residue of the circus posters, or, they speculated, did the mirrors contain actual images of apes, like magic lantern projections, but which only manifested when someone stood before them? Whatever the case, it made them feel that they lacked clear definition, that they were devoid of a perduring & definite substance, that something in them had ruptured, split, or bisected, that their genetic makeup was beginning to fragment & go haywire.

As they tried to determine if they had perceived something real or something imaginary, or if they were suffering from an infection & were unaware of it, or if there was a technological deception at work, or if their DNA was breaking down, the raucous, near-violent laughter of the kookaburras echoed throughout the building and, almost as if in chorus, or dialogue with them, the hyenas erupted into high cackling giggles and grunt-laughs. When a donkey trotted by and emitted an extended bray, its hee-haw ricocheting against the walls of the circus-jungle-library for thirty seconds, the employees wondered if the animals had escaped from local zoos and found refuge in the building, or if they had been brought there deliberately. Did one of the wandering circuses that were still about take shelter in the library during the pandemic and eventually flee, leaving the animals behind? What else would a traveling circus do, where else could it go, during a pandemic? There was no public to entertain. If so, the mirrors were possibly some kind of funhouse objects, machines or optical devices for producing the recognition of the ape. Who else would have affixed to the walls the various images of seeds *&* so on? Clearly not the birds or donkeys, clearly, not the hyenas...

Surrounding the display of pickled punks were other maps, of the world throughout history, of all of the continents of the earth from every different historical period, dating back as far as the existence of maps, making one of the librarians think of a homeless person, a former geologist, who used to regularly request documents from the map division and pin them to the wall, linking different points on each document with a series of tacks *&* threads, till the history of the world looked like a confused constellation, fractal sets gone amok, or dismantled radiolaria cast against the wall like colored spaghetti.

While she was picking up an incongruent medley of books that were scattered about — works on biology, various religious texts, studies of astronomy, evolution —, the librarian heard the sound of wheels violently rumbling across the floor.

Glancing in the direction of the noise, she saw an enormous homeless man, so dirty he didn't look human, so fetid he stank like a pestilential beast, thrusting a cart full of books out of the library.

She stood up to run after him, to stop him from stealing the books, but was terrified: he was moving far too fast, at a speed that was bewildering; in contrast, her pace seemed like stop motion. Even if she could intercede, even if she could reason with him that he did not have to steal the books, that he would always be free to read them, she would never be able to catch him.

As he rushed out the door and the noise of the cart rumbling over the ground scarred the air, she discovered that the books before her were full of voluminous marginalia, that they contained underlined words, marked off paragraphs, question marks, vehement exclamations, boldly underlined capitalized exclamations of XN!, crossed-out paragraphs, & other strange, indecipherable markings, a kind of code that she could not decipher, a language foreign to her. Held captive by the markings, while she was studying them, another librarian thought she saw an ape, or some mute, quadrupedic, hairy human, fleeing with armfuls of books, and then another, and another, and interspersed by grunts, kissing noises, and throaty, explosive calls, the strident, childlike voices of the parrots kept repeating the words, *And God said, Let us make man in our image, after our likeness*, squeak squeak, *and let them have dominion over the fish of the sea*, screech screech, *and over the fowl of the air*, ha ha, *and over the cattle, and over every creeping thing that creepeth upon the earth*, whistle whistle, *& God said unto them, be fruitful, and multiply, and replenish the earth, and subdue it*: screech screech, *ha ha*, crack-er crack-er, ha ha, ha ha, *ha haaa* ~

The mishegoss started with synagogues which, as with many other public buildings, having not been inhabited for so long due to the pandemic, suffered significant cosmetic & structural damage, damage further compounded by the destructive effects of natural disasters: shattered windows, pierced roofs, broken doors, rapidly deteriorating rafters, walls, and floors, water leaks cracking and crumbling concrete and corroding and rusting metal, generally compromising the integrity of the structures. Despite the damages largely being natural, considering the numerous strange acts of vandalism, fears abounded that synagogues had been openly targeted, and charges of anti-Semitism arose, with accusations leveled mostly against Arabs, provoking further conflicts & tensions between them and the Jews — outbreaks of extreme violence erupted in communities across the earth, against individuals and institutions, for nothing is more exulting to the species than reveling in the role of Talionis Lex!

The prolonged absence of humans and general lack of maintenance of public buildings coupled with the meteorological cataclysms made them into breeding grounds of mold, decay, and fungal rot. If dripping and stagnant water attracted flies, mosquitoes, and roaches, and wood and drywall slowly disintegrated and rotted, with frames warping, it was the influx, or incursion, a kind of covert razzia, of animals that led to furniture and other objects being gnawed, scratched, broken, or damaged in bewildering ways, with shit, piss, semen, and other animal remnants, like regurgitated cud, present everywhere. And some wondered, were there not flies, mosquitoes, and roaches in the bodies of the faithful too, and did their wood and drywall not also slowly disintegrate and rot, their frames not warp, become soiled with shit, piss, semen, and regurgitated cud?

Since the synagogues had been peopled by everything from cattle to sheep, ducks, and quail, the Jews were suspicious that the animals did not just wander into the buildings of their own accord. The event was too inexplicable, too precisely symbolic; they had to have been brought there purposely, as a statement, with Arabs and animal activists

being the main suspects, or some theological ter-
rorists working on behalf of the Vatican. Since the
entire earth was under lockdown, determining such
was difficult to prove, and in the midst of the various disasters, all surveillance systems had broken
down. The swift disintegration of their synagogues
also terrified the Jews, because it wasn't just an
isolated building that had suffered attack, but synagogues the world over, making them wonder if
the hand of God was not at work, and that perhaps
the Muslims were right, that Mohammed did come
to put an end to all religions, that Islam was the
final revelation — were all of the strange, bizarre
acts not signs that Yahweh had had enough, that
he was enacting judgment, punishment, and vengeance against the Jews for centuries of moral and
spiritual decrepitude, for an excessive and contin-
ual flouting of and corruption of religious law, or
had they just eaten too much shellfish in secret?

With the presence of fish, birds, and other live-
stock following in churches around the world, from
rams to fattened calves to spiders, locusts, and
snakes, and with churches suffering an equal or
greater degree of physical and cosmetic destruction, the Jews found it difficult to believe that their
fears were unfounded. Were they mistaken about
their faith, & would they have to become Muslims?
What was worse, having to convert to Christianity,

or to Islam? Would they not rather be atheists than have to observe halal dietary restrictions, let alone face the cross, offense of offenses? If so, they couldn't help but admit that the Arabs did have much better desserts than they did. With the discovery however of the ape-Christs, a greater number of Jews doubted that any of the strange acts were the result of the hand of God; more probably, they were the work of pranksters, provocateurs, or radical evolutionists, though the abundant presence of cats in churches led the Vatican to presume that the culprits were a coven of witches, while the thought that the Roman Catholic Empire still believed in witches made physicists the world over explode with laughter.

Yet, when it was discovered that cattle had invaded mosques around the world, and that all monotheistic buildings had become like wild menageries or savage animal terrain, it was difficult not to surmise that coordinated actions had been committed against the entire Abrahamic Empire; that some grand conspiracy was in effect. What if the vandals were physicists? Had they finally had enough of debating mythologies in public forums as if they were truths? Had they not endured one straw too many in having to pay even the slightest heed to archaic balderdash like Genesis, let alone the wrath of rabid fanatics?

After months of working to recover their buildings and clearing away debris, the Jews, Christians, and Muslims each discovered to their consternation the pervasive presence of salt in their temples of worship. Inexplicably, the more of the organic mineral they cleared away, the more it continued to appear, as if the very act of removing it led to its ever-greater generation, to it seeping through every crack, hole, and crevice of their buildings, as if reality had become a spiritual horror film, which lent further grist to the mill that a holy war was at hand, or rather, a war against the Abrahamic colonizers. Although a binder and stabilizer of foodstuffs, although it gives piquancy to discourse or writing, or liveliness to a person's character, salt was not a binder and stabilizer of spirit, let alone of buildings. If it was once regarded as having the power to repel spiritual and magickal evil, this wasn't just a saving *cum grano salis*, this was more salt than spirit could bear, this was enough salt for bread and circuses, this was enough salt for 2 million christs to season two million fish, and if he tried to pull off an even grander version of that multiplication act, there was more than enough salt to spare, enough to enable anyone to bite on whatever matter they wanted, or to spend the night amongst anyone they desired. Crystallizing inside the pores of the buildings' materials, the salt corroded stone, concrete, and brick, breaking and crumbling the walls of the structures like hungry termites. Was this the beginning of the final breaking and crumbling of metaphysical structures too, the total eradication of spirit from earth? The salt would have to erode the same structures from the soul.

While environmental forces did generate salt damage via atmospheric pollutants or groundwater, the overabundant presence of salt in those buildings clearly indicated sabotage. Later, it was discovered that, aside from salt factories and salt mines around the world having been sundered, the Dead Sea had been stripped of so much salt that its environment underwent drastic metamorphosis during the pandemic, and plants and animals started to flourish there, an alteration that led to further speculation about the anti-religious motives of the culprits behind the global crimes. It was determined that there was no metaphysical mystery, that the appearance of the salt was not an act of divine intervention, but that it was hand engineered, that a nimiety of metric tons of salt had been dropped into every crevice, hole, and crack of mosques, churches, and synagogues by design, leading to their accelerated decay, a decay exacerbated by the extreme weather conditions, with all of the buildings having become menageries of a kind: wild, savage habitats where the human no longer reigned, but the animal, where there was no

metaphysics, only physics, where there were no sermons, only baaing, quacking, and bleating, where
there were no recitations of psalms, only buzzing,
clicking, & hissing, where there was no proclaim-
ing of the ṣalāt, only lowing, bellowing, and strigu-
lating, where there was no unleavened bread, but
a hell of a lot of dung, enough for the faithful to
sit on, for a long time, because, with all of those
animals, there was endless & infinite defecation,
and of the greatest variety, too.

Having taken over, inhabited, and altered each
space to such a degree, synagogues were no longer
just synagogues, churches were no longer just churches, and mosques were no longer just mosques but,
like the libraries, they had become hybrid buildings
whose character had been forever altered — they
were now synagogue-jungles, church-forests, and
mosque-zoos, with each on the verge of becoming
nothing more than rubble, and their gods, as the
gods of the Lydians, in the midst of extinction, if
not already extinct, mere shadows persisting over
time, like light from dead stars traveling through
space, light that would eventually peter out, fading into the night like vanishing ellipses, for they
were nothing but ellipses. Did they actually believe
that their gods would last forever? And that their
civilizations would last forever? Why would they
not also peter out and die, like every previous civilization? We may with confidence anticipate, Lyell

said, that if the duration of the planet is indefinite-
ly protracted, many edifices and implements of
human workmanship & the skeletons of man will
be entombed in freshwater, marine, and volcanic
strata. None of the works of a mortal being can be
eternally; they must nevertheless eventually perish; for every year some portion of the earth's crust
is shattered by earthquakes or melted by volcanic
fire, or ground to dust by the moving waters on the
surface. The river of Lethe, as Bacon eloquently
remarked, runneth as well above ground as below.
— Yet the species continued as if death & oblivion
did not exist, as if it would never perish, and in the
face of all efforts at recovery and renovation, the
particular scent of such a host of animals remained
in every jungle-forest-zoo building, persisting as
a concrete reminder of the animal kingdom and of
all of its elements, &, despite the seeming imper-
meability of such edifices, despite the thickness of
their walls, despite their æsthetic beauty, however
turgid, morbid, or geometric, there was no barrier
between the human and the animal or plant kingdom, they were not separate, for in the face of every
bridge, in the face of every elevated structure, in
the face of every domicile, of every hedge, fence, or
blockade, nature worked its way inward, or outward,
for nature is an intelligible sphere (the only one),
whose center is everywhere, and whose circumference is nowhere, whether through its events, what

humanity called its disasters, or through its eruption in the human animal itself, out of which nature burst forth like a geyser, in the face of metaphysics and cryonics, in the face of digitalism, in the face of graveyards & monuments, manifesting in a whorl of guises, or concealed by humanity with its very own guises, but what could not be concealed was the relation between the human, the hominid, and the ape, and in the basements of the synagogues, churches, and mosques, or whatever they had become, in the new jungles, forests, and zoos around the world, interlocking skeletons of apes, humans, and hominids had been found and there was very little difference between them.

Centered high on a wall, when first being commandeered into the laboratory, the subjects noticed a quote that had been scrawled in perfect script, broken up as if it were verse, the final two words angled to imitate italic text:

> Man still bears
> in his bodily frame
> the indelible stamp
> of his *lowly origin*.

> Charles Darwin
> *The Descent*
> *of Man*

Adjacent to the quote was a drawing of coral with a variety of branches riven into multitudinous directions, some ending, some continuing, some wider than the ones below them, each moving in erratic directions; to its left, starting at the top of the ceiling and spanning the expanse of the entire laboratory, were images of the process of evolution, ending, in the final room, at least at this point in the timescale of the earth, with homo sapiens. The chain began with immense images of self-replicating RNA molecules, Prokaryotes, and Cyanobacteria, then proceeded to Eukaryotes, Choanoflagellates, and Epithelia, whose mouths, muscles, connective nerve tissue, & photoreceptive eye-spots were emphasized in detail, marked as if a significant stage in its journey, one outcome of which was homo sapiens — perhaps, some wondered, as distant in time as Epithelia were, the species hadn't progressed so far. While rubbing her hands over her breasts, *I feel*, one of the subjects said to herself, *very epithelic today.*

As they were forced into the next chamber, the images continued, with Urbilaterians, Deuterostomes, Platyhelminthes, and Pikaia, whose spines & post-anal tails had been enlarged — there were multiple images of those parts, depicted from diverse angles, denoting various features, in exploded close-up, all of which contained precise markings & measurements. When being marched thru the laboratory, reflexively, some people furtively reached behind themselves to feel their tailbones, as if checking for the remains of a post-anal appendage, or wondering if, in the interim, one had possibly started to form. Was it an urban legend, what they were told when they were young, that some people are still born with miniature tails and that doctors removed & discarded them?

Meandering along, the shift from Unicellular life to the Multicellular life of Animalia progressed to a series of Chordata, the backboned animals complete with ears, camera eyes, & pineal glands, beneath which was a note:

If Descartes is correct about the pineal gland, is this then not the onset of the soul, the instance of its first appearance?? Is the Agnatha not the first "souled-creature"??

The fact that it could see & hear, that it had skin layers, a two-chambered heart, and the ability to taste, lent weight to the hypothesis, particularly because taste, that is, as an epistemic and moral concept, represents a spiritualization of animality. Was it not therefore the beginning of the war with animality, an inner split, schism, & self-destructive seed, the heart cracking into halves, developing separate chambers, bifurcating the animal, cultivating its future desire for cutlery? Although Haikouichthys had brains, blood, branched blood vessels, pharynxes, and the ability to smell, despite their possible vocalic capacities, their lack of pineal glands rendered them no more than tertiary creatures. The birth of the soul had to have begun with Agnatha, and when first depicting an image of it, early man drew it with agnathic features. That its pharyngeal slits became gills revealed the archaic icthyodic aspects of the human species, not to speak of the fishiest aspects of Catholicism.

Moving along the wall like the inevitable progression of time, zigzagging without relent, the images continued, with Placodermi which, in being the first species with a spleen and adaptive immunity, was perchance the creature in whom the figure of the modern poet had its primary origin. In examining it more closely, it was difficult not to discern a resemblance between Placodermi & Baudelaire. Why a thesis had yet to be written on such Vertebrata and *poètes maudits* was baffling, for it would give great insight into the many difficulties of poiesis, but then, of what concern is poetics — as Luca said, there is no place in this world for Placodermi, and, as Hölderlin said before him, my heart already belongs to the dead.

Following the ancestor of the poet was the Cephalaspis and the Cœlacanth, which closed out the line of Chordata, but not their future, for it would coral off into many other taxa, cleaving into the most unsuspected of lines, from Lampreys to Amphibia and Archosauromorpha. Homo sapiens remained extremely remote, but with the evolution of the Panderichthys, the first Tetrapoda, in some way, the species was impending, for the protolimbs of that creature would eventually evolve into legs, such as with the Tiktaalik, seemingly the first animal to walk on land. It was time to get the hell out of the sea & start looking around, especially with a soul in the making — that thing had ambitions: there were gods to invent, religions to establish, fish to catch.

The line of development from the Tiktaalik to the Acanthostega was obvious, the visual evidence clear to a child, as was the development from it to the Ichthyostega which, with its tear glands, could be the first instance, the original seed, of the tragedian, demonstrating that Placodermi came first, that the poet was the first human type to be seeded in the evolutionary catena — black bile before phlegm, melancholy before anguish, it's perfectly logical. *You can't lament without a spleen...*

Next came the Pederpes: with its tongue, salivary glands, three-chambered heart, glottis, & bladder, it was difficult not to recognize it as the onset of the hypochondriac, those uncritical creatures with an intense disposition to believe — there it was, staring them in the face, the reptilian ancestor of the monotheist. In losing dorsal, anal, and tail fins, how could it not be less perspectivally adept, its agnathic optics more cyclopic than peacockian? And what else but a creature with a three-chambered heart would give birth to a mania for trinities, cleaving the species into a tripartite, spirit-obsessed, geometrically imbalanced animal, like an old man hobbling along with a cane? It's a biological illness, one of the subjects thought to herself, an accident of evolution, and the ironies of its name did not escape her. The Tetrapoda came to a close with the Westlothiana and the Hylonomus which, with its adrenal glands and lack of gills, was the tetrapodic antecedent of the industrialist — with the loss of the gill system, which remained as an obstreperous, itchy ghost organ continually troubling the species, it developed an antipathy toward oceans and seas, bodies of water it would regularly devastate out of contempt for its archaic past, its adrenal gland releasing floods of steroid hormones, agitating the nerves, provoking destructive tempests of action.

Turning into another darker chamber of the laboratory, the subjects came upon images of the Mammalia line, moving from the Phthinosuchus to the Cynognathus which, in being free of a pineal gland, should have unbound the coming species of the spiritual impulse, but, somehow, that damn thing would make its way back into the genetic makeup. The Repenomamus followed, illustrating that evolution did not entail progressive, linear development, or advancement from a lower to a higher type, for Placodermi were clearly superior to creatures whose vision went from tetrochromatic to dichromatic, its ocular scope narrowing to thinner and thinner spectrums, closing out more & more of reality, operating through obreption, eschewing more and more of the sensory world, a world which, eventually, the species would long hold in derision, relegating the material realm & all of its inhabitants immaterial, inferior to the ephemeral and spectral realm of metaphysics. The formation of forward-facing eyes, and so the ever greater reduction of optics, began with primates, the very order of mammals that homo sapiens would refuse to see in its rearview mirror since, in constructing a metaphysics, it worked to obscure and erase its material lineage through the most extraordinary, bewitching, and phantasmagoric forms of obreption, an indication of reptilian impulses taking conceptual form. Was it the combination of diurnality and menstruation, seeing the raw material of life in broad daylight, that led to its horror of itself?

And with the loss of its tail, could the emerging species no longer face its primitive past, with it beginning to feel revulsion for its animal heritage? Feeling a little bump above her ass, one woman wondered if, late in life, just as hairs & other things begin to appear in unsuspecting places on the body, a tail could not also possibly emerge. If so, would someone with a tail have the effrontery to continue to prostrate herself before an altar?

As they were forced deeper into the laboratory, which became darker and darker with every turn, the sole light in the space limited to a lantern illuminating the images, when passing by a variety of Hominidæ, as they came face to face with immense pictures of Ouranopithecus, Orrorin, Ardipithecus, and Australopithecus, the low, muffled noise of broods of plucked fowl sounded in the distance, the clamor of their scurrying feet rising in volume as the light of the lantern flickered across the images. Hundreds of small gates clicked open, one after another, in rapid-fire succession, making a violent commotion like the rat-a-tat-tat of a machine gun magazine being unloaded, and fowl after fowl ran by the feet of the subjects, a terrifying horde of them, clucking, hissing, growling, the noises piercing their eardrums, their voices intensified via amplification, which replayed and multiplied the clucks, hisses, and growls of the biped

& featherless animals, all reverberating throughout the laboratory, echoing against its chambers,
the noises growing infinitely pronounced as the
subjects were led into a room with a series of microscopes and almost entirely void of light. When
forced to put their eyes to the lenses, the focused
beam of illumination emerging from within the
instrument temporarily blinded them. Their eyes
having adjusted, as the lenses of the instrument
focused, as the sound of fire crackled in the air *&*
the temperature of the room increased to over 100°,
the images they saw formed into clearer *&* clearer
shapes, images that is of the Genus Homo, each
smaller than the next, with Homo Erectus the larg-
est of the micro images, Homo Neanderthalensis
less so, and homo sapiens even more minuscule,
the most difficult of the series to discern. Strange-
ly, the last image kept going in and out of focus,
losing definition, its edges growing fuzzy, its form
breaking down, till it finally disappeared altogether. Were the lenses of the microscopes broken? Was
the image defective? Were the dichromatic eyes of
the subjects beginning to fail them? Or had they
unknowingly been administered some drug before
entering the laboratory, a gas that permeated the
air, its effect escalating with each step farther and
farther inward, or whatever direction it was they
were being moved?

In the midst of their deliberations, intermingled with the clucking, hissing, and growling fowl, the subjects heard a strange, basso profondo voice, even deeper it seemed than an oktavist, reciting, they say, *the solid earth whereon we tread in tracts of fluent heat began, and grew to seeming-random forms, the seeming prey of cyclic storms, till at the last arose the man; who throve & branch'd from clime to clime, the herald of a higher race, and of himself in higher place, if so he type this work of time within himself, from more to more; or, crown'd with attributes of woe like glories, move his course, and show that life is not as idle ore but iron dug from central gloom, and heated hot with burning fears, and dipt in baths of hissing tears, and batter'd with the shocks of doom to shape and use. Arise and fly the reeling faun, the sensual feast; move upward, working out the beast, and let the ape and tiger die...*

Move up-ward, the voice repeated, this time stated as if a question, as if the action was doubtful, as if one could not but be skeptical of it, as if it were a fallacy, the last syllable of the final word dissolving amidst the growing noise of the clucking, hissing, growling fowl, the sound of crackling fire dying down, sizzling out to silence.

Move upward, the basso profondo voice repeated again, working out the beast, *AND LET THE TIGER AND APE DIE*, the voice bellowed, ever more full of question, its tone violent, fierce, not a lamentation, but a howl, a brutal, wild, primitive growl.

From the ground and above, legions of monkeys and hyenas emerged, peering out of pet doors and from miniature balconies, accompanying the basso profondo condemnation with a chorus of laughter, at which point, each of the subjects were seized, corralled into an operating theater, and bound to autopsy tables.

As they twitched *&* jerked in vain attempts to escape, some thought to themselves, were they within the iron hills referred to in the radio broadcast?

Although they could not turn their heads, the subjects heard the sound of surgical tools being carefully arranged in instrument trays. The surgeons then applied speculums with open wire loops to the subjects' eyes to retract their eyelids.

All light in the operating theater went out.

In the absolute blackness, above their heads, a hypnotic film fluttered forth on the ceiling, an amalgamation of images, sometimes text, sputtering through the projector at varying speeds, depicting over 300,000 species of Plants, ending with the title card:

450 GIGATONS OF CARBON

82.4% OF BIOMASS ON EARTH

then exploding into kaleidoscopic images of Bacteria fused with images of Fungi & Archæa, shifting into Protists, then Marine Arthropods, the images not contained in a fixed, square frame, but moving outward, across the space, onto the bodies of the subjects: Crabs, Lobsters, Shrimp, Sea Spiders each traversing space-time as if moving through water, Barnacles beginning to appear on the bodies of the subjects, till they were nearly covered in them, their feet, hands, and groins encrusted with images of Barnacles, after which Sharks, Swordfish, and Eels moved through the room, then evaporated, the light of the images of them fading to darkness, as if disintegrating, with 22,000 species of Annelids emerging before them: Clitellata, Leeches, Palpata, Sedentaria, and Errantia, all of which evaporated too, the light of their images vanishing, fading into oblivion, till the room was dominated by images of Terrestrial Arthropods, the Barnacled bodies of the subjects besieged by 0.2 Gigatons of Carbon of Centipedes, Spiders, Scorpions, and Tongue Worms, with an equal tonnage of images of Mollusks sprouting over their brains & groins: Snails, Slugs, Squid, & a variety of Octopods, seemingly exuded from their pores, but they too swiftly dissipated, like light from sputtering candles, the space again going completely dark, and in the blackness, in the darkest inky blackness, as the eyes of the subjects began to grow dry, itch, and burn, as their bodies became entirely encased in Barnacles, save for their propped open eyes, images of 0.2 Gigatons of Carbon of Viruses surged forth from the projectors, seething through space-time, organisms at the edge of life, mingled in complex & multitudinous ways with the Dura images, slaughterhouses, then more Viruses, fish, anchors, shepherds & oil spills, then yet other Viruses, out of which images and sounds of Amazon wildfires flared, some scenes dissolving, fading into one another, overlapping, washing one another out, disintegrating, as if the film were being eaten up or burned away, as if it were undergoing combustion, each image soon being overwritten by fourfold Muhammad in geometric script & asbestos clouds, then an illustration of Muhammad with an entirely veiled face, his hands upheld before him, his body surrounded by a rising flame out of which burst images of freshwater and marine Cnidarians: Jellyfish, Sea Anemones, and Siphonophores, coupled with the sound of Pigs, Cows, Chickens, Goats, & Honeybees, images of which then appeared in the room, interspersed with scenes of oil fires, chemical plant explosions, nuclear disasters and their respective noises, the flickering, spectral flashes of Chickens mixing with the real fowl clucking, hissing, and growling outside the operating theater, each too swiftly disappearing, like light from a laser going dark, the room too going dark, darker than ever, a black blacker than any night, a black devoid of all light, into which sputtered microscopic images of homo sapiens, which, despite their being only a minuscule portion of the biomass of the earth, dominated the room, spit out of the projector with photonic velocity, like shards of splintered glass from a woodchopper, the light from the projectors fizzling out, burning away like dying comets, the room entirely black, numbers, letters, decimal points, manifesting one by one on the bodies of the subjects, painting over them:

0, then a decimal point, then another 0, then a 6, then a G, then an I, then another G, then an A, T, O, and N, each number and letter burnt into their bodies with extreme heat, like branding irons marking cattle:

S, O, F, some letters scarred, some shattered and split, forming in pieces, bit by bit, the cutting horizonal line of an H, the hard blunt bar of an A, the vertiginous precipices of a V, the infinite, prolapsed void of a bursting O, the threatening, open maw of a C, its teeth digging into knees, hooking onto spines, the teeming void of another prolapsed O encircling an eye, the sharp, beveled edges of an N embedded in an esophagus, the lethal blades of an L searing an earlobe, some letters & numbers appearing dispersed across entire bodies:

a Y here, a 0 there, a decimal point elsewhere, another o imprinted over the aorta, a needle-like 1 scored into the folds of the flesh of their genitals, a percentage mark with its double zeros & dividing precipice emblazoned on X-marked foreheads, the fowl continuing to cluck, hiss, and growl while yet more letters are dispersed over the bodies of the subjects:

O's, F's, B's, I's, whereas others are scored together in single places on the flesh:

MASS

and as the laughter of the monkeys & hyenas grew hysterical, the final letters:

ON EARTH

were tattooed across wrists to the amplified sound of captive bolt pistols and their concussive blows, and when the eyelids or cornea of some subjects were touched, many of them continued to blink, while others exhibited righting reflexes, their legs twitching, their heads not hanging straight down and limp, but staring straight ahead, their bodies barnacled, save for the sliver of open eyes and crack of pinnæ, as lipstick'd, mascara'd monkeys in space suits whispered in their ears: *futile & frail monster, dream and discord, the final law shrieks against your creed...*

Ruins, ruins, everywhere ruins: dust, decay, debris, the detritus of civilization, of devastated cities, of a cloistered planet set into a severe cæsura, of a nearly voided earth, of downed communication lines, of a species submerged in conflict, with some warring faction relentlessly aggressing against it and yet evading detection, known only to those who had been directly subjected to its actions but who had not escaped its hold. Under occupation, in the midst of this protracted & inexorable state of oblivion, reality itself seemed dubitable, it too in a state of ruin or disintegration, as was life on earth — it was as if something was pushing the species to surpass, supersede, or eradicate itself, some force, whether phusis itself, telluric elements, or a specific agent or organized faction. Fears emerged that a despot was staging a new grand world war and that the experiments being conducted were initial forays into assaults that would grow ever more terrifying & pervasive; others believed that aliens were engineering the eerie & catastrophic events. Who else could operate on such a global scale & evade detection? The more sober minded conjectured that the planet was entering a highly accelerated evolutionary shift, spurred into effect by cosmological incidents that had yet to be discerned. As much as the species generally forgot, the earth was a planet within a Milky Way whose forces had regular minor and large-scale effects upon it. Whatever was at work, the ruination and fear plunged legions of people into intractable existential crises, crises that struck at the cellular, axonal, & circulatory levels. Ambivalent over how to reassure themselves that they were human and nothing but human & that reality & life on earth would perdure, they fled to mirrors to gaze at themselves, to secure their identity by testing their perception, by looking into mirrors to see themselves, to see the return of their reflections and nothing else, to see the firm outlines of their bodies, their faces, their gestures. But was the mirror reflecting and returning something actual and solid, or was it liquid, fluid, mutating, in fact a threatening or dangerous object? Did it reflect reality, concrete reality, or only consciousness in continuous phantomatic play, like the flitting, shifting frames of a film which, if slowed down enough, would not reveal what the legions thought they were seeing, but something else altogether? Was not the mirror returning a semblance of truth, or truth itself? Was it not plain, factual, dry, like the cold, sober light of an operating table? Is there not a firm distinction between the real and the imaginary that the mirror reinforces? Or is it the realm where fantasy and imagination erupt, surge forth, and explode, like subtle specters, phantasms that confuse and obfuscate since they do not resemble phantasms but bare reality? The space-time where dream and reality fuse, with each dissipating to such a degree that one cannot be distinguished from the other? Are they not seeing what they are seeing, that is, are they not seeing what is real, tangible, factual, or is the subconscious depicting its subterranean reality, and if so, is that real or a mutation? Is it a mere flashing picture of the mind, a quotidian hallucination with the appearance of reality, or is it reality? When they thrust their hands forward into the glass, they thought that nothing was there, that it was only water, or air, through which they were testing the surface — then they realized that they were only imagining that they were thrusting their hands into the mirror: they were far enough away from it that their extended limbs did not touch the surface, that it was only a perceptual distortion they were experiencing, as if, in the midst of the day, in the midst of regular consciousness, they had shifted in and out of dream consciousness, a daydream, a day distortion, a day hallucination, as if they were on peyote, or emerging from a powerful reverie, drifting in and out of consciousness from moment to moment with such intensity that, what they were envisioning with their minds, or what their minds were projecting, or what their minds were detecting … they could not determine what was what —

it blended with such intensity, speed, & accuracy that each moment they seemed to return to reality they weren't sure if it was reality, dream, hallucination, fantasy, or perceptual distortion. A flash of fire; a biblioclasm; an ape. I have said to the worm, thou art my mother & my sister. *Where did these words that just entered their minds come from?* They felt them emerge like an incursion; like an entirely foreign, strange, disquieting thought that entered them like an alien agent manifesting at the nerve level. It was a sensation & form of cogitation not their own. It felt as if something else was suddenly breathing inside of them, as if their blood was pulsing differently, as if the cores of their bodies were being penetrated from deep within. Was it a symptom and sign of an infection, or merely the subconscious wreaking havoc with their sanity? Did the prolonged removal or separation from what they considered reality distort their relation to reality or everyday perception to such a degree that they could no longer distinguish between the real & the irreal, or, in being removed from the din of everyday activity, did they actually begin to finally see reality for what it was? Did their excision from the social theater open them to the wild, spooky stream of reality itself, a reality that no longer required microscopes, infrared lenses, or other optical devices to be seen, but which was plainly visible and present, as if the subatomic domain became atomic, as if the distortion of human perception finally cracked apart, as if the frames of consciousness had shattered and they were seeing reality at the pace of dragonflies, or at the speed of light? Is some autonomous & menacing double usurping the true reflection of themselves, or is reality finally breaking into reality, that is, *breaking through the screen of consciousness's delusory patina*? Is it illusion taking on substance, or is illusion substance, the true substance that consciousness disrupts? Standing stock-still, gazing again into the mirror, they sought to fix objects, to see concrete things, to locate things in space & time: here is Y, there is X. No, *the real is real* — there are walls, there are floors, there are ceilings, there are doors. Even if nothing is solid & concrete at the subatomic level, that is not the level on which quotidian reality functions, that is not the totality of the real, they reassured themselves. *Reality is reality*. The subatomic is like metaphysics; it is elsewhere; what is here is here. And reaching out again to feel the surface of the mirror, their fingers met their fingers, their gazes met their gazes, their gestures matched their gestures, their actions were each replicated: eyes blinking when they blinked, mouths opening simultaneously, reflection and self, self and reflection, all bound together, all real, the mirror screaming when they screamed, the glass shattering when they shattered. A precise unity: dream was dream; reality was reality. The psychic world & the exterior world do not cross, save for in the dream. Each remains distinct, each retains its thresholds, each has its supporting structures & frames. Illusion remains illusion & is only delusion when it is mistaken for the real — one steps from the plank of the ship in the sea of one's dream into one's bedroom, not into any watery depths. The terror of the shark when there is no shark is the terror of the imagination — *it is psychosis*. If what was what was not what however, was it merely the disintegration of consciousness, a shift into some other state, or had legions of people undergone some physical transformation set into effect by aliens, or a metaphysical or cosmological incident? When they began to no longer be able to see themselves as themselves, what were they any longer? Was it not in fact dangerous to look into mirrors for too long? Did it not eventually present distortions? Did something not begin to crack with too lengthy a gaze? Or was reality finally presenting itself as itself at last? A flash of fire; a biblioclasm; an ape. I have said to the worm, thou art my mother & my sister. Again the incursion came: that swift, that unexpected, like being struck in the face with a gust of wind on a stagnant day, or like a bolt of lightning hitting ground on a sun-filled afternoon, as if some other entity were thinking inside of them, as if they were being penetrated from afar, and it was schismatic, like they were speaking two different languages at once, as if the thought manifesting within them was being spoken in one language, or some form of language entirely extrinsic to them: barbaric, savage, feral, while the words that were articulated, as if via ventriloquism, were in their native tongue. Feeling the presence of something in their midst, as if thought were presence, they turned violently to and fro, rushing from *&* then returning to their mirrors as if they were securing anchors or ballasting walls and not quicksand. What were those strange apparitions they saw when quickly walking by and glancing back into the mirror? An image that did not look like themselves but strangers, monsters, beasts. In gazing too long into the mirror, does one not finally move beyond the surface of the image and into its depth, into its reality? It is not that the surface lacks depth, but that one doesn't look long enough into the surface to see, reveal, and unfold its depth. Were they then not seeing the true depths of their surfaces? Were they finally seeing reality itself? Was the shimmering only a mirage, or was it subatomic reality, the real of the real breaking away from without and into quotidian consciousness? The *Ding an sich* going *ding,*

ding, ding in their heads like clappers till the bells broke into pieces. Did the volatile capriciousness of the reflective world take on agency and perma- nence, become more solid and perduring? Is the flash not a flash but something moving so fast that homo sapiens continually lose sight of it, capturing it only for an instant, thinking a flash is only or merely a flash, when in fact it is simply something moving at a speed beyond anthropomorphic per- ceptual capacities, and their ever seeing it in the first place is but a lucky acquisition, a crack into an other temporality beyond the normal purview of the species, as if the mind instantaneously and by accident, through some genetic mishap or anoma- lous event, leapt into a more highly evolved state for an instant and then came crashing back to X and Y. Were they looking into mirrors, or did the mirrors become veiled computer screens that imi- tated, with slight distortions, their own bodies? Were they seeing another body, another entity, or their own body as another entity, another species even, something in chrysalis? What was this dis- turbing thought about the worm? What was that other form of cogitation that entered them from afar and was being opened within them, taking hold like a parasite, virus, or host? Were they look- ing at mirrors, or through some form of glass that seemed like a mirror but which wasn't and which replicated but slightly mutated their every gesture, a matching but distorting film that fused with their consciousness to such a degree that confused their ability to discern that what was what was what? Did the body itself become an optical machine through which the archaic chain of the species and its efflorescence was made manifest, visible to the normal eye, a transmutation of the entirety of time unfolding in swift but visible motion? Or was it a catoptric aberration, some paralogical event or natural anamorphosis, the perceptual apparatus gone spooky & prismatic? When plants, rocks, atmospheric elements & other non-human matter overtook their bodies, seemingly sprouting from them like living tendrils, the legions started to have a thought emerge in their minds: it wasn't that, with unveiled faces, they were beholding as in a mirror the glory of the Lord and being transformed into the same image from glory to glory, but that they were being decomposed into disaggregated elements, and so they were plunged into catatonic states, rendered altogether other & mute.

The playing field is littered with human and animal remains, and vases, altars, obelisks, & broken symbols of power are scattered about the skulls & bones. Dense grey clouds hang over the devastated wasteland and an owl is perched in a high tree, as if watching over, surveying, or guiding the game, which began with the eternal pounding of waves on the shore & continued on the high mountaintop in the jungle, in the deep shadows that lie like specters on such great summits, & with each film, with each foray into the history of the species, the night grew more impenetrable & dark.

Throughout the game, the sound of the sea was heard from afar, its vibratory resonances entering the jungle, & so touching the mountaintop, making itself present sonically, as if there were no firm demarcating boundary between earth & sea, whose innumerable points, threads, and surfaces surged forth into vegetable life — through intensification, vast tracts of sea turned impure, turbid, slimy, its surface breaking out into phosphorescent light, the *Noctiluca scintillans* sailors call sea sparkle. While this luminosity is present in fish and other creatures, the whole surface of the sea, too, is partly an infinite shining, partly an immeasurable, immense sea of light, and an equally immeasurable, immense spray of scintillating light of another kind flickered forth from the squares of the surface of the empty chessboard, each of which, like visionary portals, became frames through which the players watched different periods of the history of humanity unfold.

Upon player one touching square 8D, the first film was activated, the quick flash of a knife sharpened, glistening, drawn across the organ, making the scar of scars, the mark of Abraham, excising the præputium, the sparest, most economical recognition of divine ownership of human life, the weakening of the organ to put it in as quiet a state as possible, a pound of flesh sacrificed to save the soul, the onset of the disaster of disasters, the world become opprobrium, the slave rebellion in morals.

As the players watched the skin fall to the earth, a fragment of flesh whose weight was immeasurable and which would reverberate through time like the aftereffects of a nuclear weapon, a strident voiceover surged from the chessboard, the final frame of the film flickering out, all light dissipating in concordance with the vehemence of the pronouncement, *"The body must be beaten down and earnest prayer made for the gift of continency!"*

After witnessing this event, the low, quiet sound of laughter, which softly increased in volume until it became a full, hearty, resounding guffaw, emerged from player one, who was brightly garbed.

Seizing a monkey, he and his cohorts reenacted the event, the sharpened knife glistening, ready to make the scar of scars, the beginning of man's dominion over all the animals, yet, just as player one was about to draw the knife across the primate's organ, he interrupted the gesture & it was set free

— the monkey bound across the earth, his every gesture pregnant with intent.

On an adjacent chessboard, player one enacted the initial move of the game, moving the rank and file across the ranks and files, crisscrossing light and dark squares, his play not dictated by personal will, choice, or strategy, but informed strictly by his interpretation of the witnessed event. Was it a self-defeating, annihilatory move, one that would bring it and everything else in its midst directly to its prolonged, living destruction?

Upon player two touching square 1A, the second film was activated, the quick flash of a knife, the head of a victim lifted up, its throat sliced, blood gushing onto an altar, the body of an animal cut open, entrails, liver, and other parts, the tablets of the gods, excised and interpreted, or burned and read by the augury-seeking manteis, who then stripped bones of flesh, covered them with fat, herbs, and spices, & burned them, the sweet-smelling smoke rising toward the gods, while other morsels were put on spits, roasted, and consumed by the seers & their acolytes.

Although they believed themselves to be separate from the animal kingdom, did they not unknowingly become part sheep, part bird, or part goat in consuming such flesh? Once their diet became carnivorous, were they then no longer strictly human, but as animal as the animals that ate other animals, or as animal as carnivorous plants?

After witnessing this event, the low, quiet sound of weeping, which softly increased in volume until it became a deep, crippling lament, emerged from player two, who was garbed in a black tunic. Before he could consider making a move, he leaned upon a stone, paralyzed by pessimism, forlorn of hope, and wept, his eyes wet with tears.

Laughing, player one ordered the scientists to practice extispicy & empyromancy on the subjects taken from the iron hills, a host of whom were set upon altars and, just as the sheep, goats, & birds, had their heads lifted, throats sliced, & bodies cut open, their entrails, livers, and other parts excised and interpreted, or burned & read, every other aspect of the ritual ceremony performed to completion, yet after trying to consume the roasted flesh, the scientists spit it from their mouths — it was not as savory as tenderloin, let alone lamb or goat.

Rising from the stone and going to the adjacent chessboard, player two enacted the second move of the game, advancing a pawn two squares, from 2F to 4F, his play also not dictated by personal will, choice, or strategy, but informed strictly by his interpretation of the witnessed events, another gesture advancing the playing field further into a state of living destruction.

In working through the inspection of human viscera, the scientists thought that the future would appear clearer, since, in being *parlêtre*, the human being is the word creature, the logos-impacted monster, the speaking animal par excellence, but the future was not more lucid, and the extracted entrails, full of nothing but deeply calcified ordure, were muddled and difficult to decipher — was that symbolic, a signifier perhaps of a coming amorphousness, of an eventual erasure?

The sheer unending mass of words accumulated over time was astonishing, a kind of mad, logorrheic effusion, but the scientists sifted through as many of the principal texts of their civilization as they could, having seized them from libraries around the world during the pandemic, the playing field of the mountaintop littered not only with human and animal remains, but with the remains of books from a multitude of centuries, spanning ancient, medieval, and modern epochs, scattered at their feet like discarded weapons, the props of a tragic trilogy in the midst of its denouement.

Gazing up at the owl, then back toward the subjects before him, player two whispered, Do you not hear behind every word the laughter of error, of imagination, of the spirit of delusion? *When you can become an animal, you will be invited into the science of the real* — that day will be superior to the day of your birth.

Shifting its head fro and to, the owl gazed with its clear, bright, piercing eyes into the distance, scanning the entire surrounding area and emitting deep, soft vocalizations: *hoo-h'HOO-hoo-hoo*, then, shifting its eyes back downward as the game commenced, it gazed intently at the board.

In touching square 8G, player one activated the third film, a nail piercing ankles, hands tied to posts, a body exposed to elements, breathing impeded, lungs obstructed by the falling weight of the body, incremental loss of breath, larynx crushed, suffocation, the crime of an agitator, religio-political insurrection mythicized, the tortured man, the sacrificed son, emblazoned in the mind through centuries of hagiography, a blitzkrieg of image after brutal image securing the gospel, horrid visual chronotopes reinforcing the ascetic ideal, refusing the archeological record, cutting a pavlovian reflex into the flesh, myth overtaking reality, usurping love of the world *&* the things in the world, horror of horrors, bane of scientists, doctors, and thinkers, bane of women, bane of the body, bane of the earth, colonizing force par excellence.

Before this divine comedy, player one and his cohorts took up axes and began chopping away at a close cluster of three nearby trees, hacking at a multitude of their limbs, stripping the plants bare until each resembled a cross, whereupon they seized another monkey, dragged it to the central cross, pierced the animal's ankles to the base, tied its hands to the outlying posts, then seized two subjects taken from the iron hills, dragging one to the cross to the left, and a second to the cross to the right of the monkey, pierced the ankles of the subjects, then tied their hands to the outlying posts.

Standing back, the player et alia contemplated the spectacle, watching as the monkey's breath started to fail, and the breath of the two subjects started to fail, the lungs of each obstructed by the falling weight of their bodies, one of them saying to the monkey just before its larynx was about to be crushed by the force of gravity drawing its body downward, "*Are you not the...*," but the monkey's larynx was not crushed, for its body was more light and lithe, and it was limber enough to extract its hands from the binds, which it did, and while gripping a post with one free hand, the animal reached down, grabbed the head of the nail that had been banged into its feet, extracted it with ease, then released himself from the mortal comedy.

Joining player one and his cohorts, the monkey watched as, their larynxes now almost entirely closed off, the two subjects endured a long, slow, incremental loss of breath, their bodies jerking, twisting, in frenetic spasm, until, finally, poundage of heavy flesh & bone dragging their bodies yet further downward, their larynxes being crushed, their final, halted breaths rattling out, breath by stunted breath, fine, high-pitched sputtering noises: life clicking, bubbling, crackling out like foam from an epileptic's mouth, till they resembled giant, mutilated, sagging Ys, dead letters soon to be absorbed, engulfed by the robust trees & forest growth below.

In the midst of their suffocating, the monkey scampered off, laughing into the trees, while player one chuckled mischievously, softly, whispering aloud, as if to everything around him, observing, *in* ... 'brutis' — he pronounced the word full of question — ... *plura observentur, quæ humanum sagacitatem longe superant?*

On the adjacent chessboard, he then enacted the next move of the game, another gesture advancing toward blindness, annihilation, and terror, toward self and world-evisceration, the socio-political climate made exceedingly grim.

Upon touching square 1E, player two activated the fourth film, an orphan meditating in a cave in the mountains, the hot August sun, the disorienting desert heat, a revelation?, the word *Read!,* a command, shouted as if from elsewhere, to which the orphan responded, *I cannot!,* and again a voice from elsewhere commanding, *Read!,* and again the illiterate objecting, *I cannot!,* and on this goes, back & forth, a see-saw of internal-dialogue, words clanging against one another like crossing swords, an illiterate madman in his most incandescent bloom, delirious, in the darkness, his projecting subconscious becoming an ethereal voice commanding absolutism and submission, for the species cannot direct itself or live in concord with its instincts, he will teach by the pen, he will teach men that which they do not know, he will teach mythology instead of investigation, he will teach fable & spiritual prestidigitation, he will inculcate sharī'ah, the body will suffer, the soul will suffer, the earth will suffer, for from him breaks forth the flame of the madness of revenge, a planet, a civilization, under the tyrannical will of an illiterate orphan, mistaking his dæmon for a deity, turning it into God.

Like a child toying with objects it does not understand, player one picked up a series of letter blocks and, randomly, haphazardly, gleefully, began mixing them up, juggling them about, throwing them here and there, staring confusedly at them, casting them like giant colored dice upon the ground, and in gazing at the outcome, commanded the animals around him, then picking up the blocks and casting them a second time, in gazing at the outcome, even though he could not read the words, he commanded the subjects around him, setting forth laws of governance, ordering social, political, and economic realms, then picking the blocks up and casting them a third time, in gazing at the outcome, even though he could not read the words, he claimed that they were irrefutable, that they were divine, that they could be disputed only by death or mutilation, and so the illiterate blood clot gazed about and commanded all of space & time and condemned the earth out of which he was issued and was declared a prophet.

Player one gazed up at the owl, then back down at the confused array of blocks, & after arranging them into a series of words, he and the owl locked eyes, seemed to communicate to one another telepathically, but remained silent, and out of their silence a silence such as had never been known hitherto on earth pervaded the atmosphere, billowed through it like a powerful magnetic wave, resounding through the air, everything momentarily quieted, still, soundless, save for the susurrating music of waves, which touched the mountaintop from afar, the ends of the lips of the crests of water unfolding like a ceaseless series of eternally curling s's: *s-s—s-s-s—s-s—s*

As player two contemplated the events they saw flickering forth from the chessboard and in the air before them, player one scrambled the blocks into a new chaos of letters and rising above the music of the waves, the low, quiet sound of weeping was

heard once again as player two, forlorn of hope
and ever more paralyzed by melancholy, stood before the ranks and files, a tapestry of time, a thick
globule of a tear falling from his eye & striking a
pawn, which began to sizzle, as if his tear was made
of acid, disfiguring the piece, which he then moved
to its inevitable position, as if some irrevocable
force, not a wave, not the wind, not gravity, but an
invented force, a concocted instinct forged & cut
into the flesh, was commanding its movement.

Turning from the game, crestfallen to the point
of near-paralysis, player two traipsed through the
detritus of the playing field and began collecting
stone after stone, which he then surrounded himself with, sitting before a pile of them as if they
were companions, stacking one on top of another
to wall himself in & to close off the world.

To the percussive sound of his array of stones,
player one listened as if to a song, to a rhythm, to
a propulsive beat, as if it were music to accompany
some great event that would later be enacted, and
in the midst of remnants of spiritual books that
had been incinerated, he began arranging and examining a series of fossils, laughing heartily as he
positioned the bones before him, contemplating
the formation of the human species and its failure
to use its senses and to recognize its limitations,
heeding mostly the first Delphic imperative, rarely

ever the second, and so remaining forever imbalanced, in extreme discord with itself and the world, a result he thought of losing contact & unity with its animal heritage.

As a worm crawled through the earth before him, he watched it meandering to & fro, burrowing in and out of the earth, pursuing a drive, its movement provoking in him an idea as he gazed around at the dizzying array of magisterial fossils, from Venericardia to Paradoxides to Radiolaria, struck by the geometric beauty of their form, of the majesty of matter, of the slow work of time.

While player two continued amassing stones, player one directed the scientists to take more subjects from the iron hills & to set them upon operating tables, & so, subject after subject was brought from captivity, firmly bound and lightly etherized, their bodies awake enough to experience sensation, but subdued enough not to twitch.

In the midst of this staging, an ambush of tigers & a shrewdness of apes emerged from the jungle, watching as the subjects each received a tattoo of a fossil on their chests, their flesh carved into with albatross bone uhi, the sound of the clicking stones of player one echoed by the sound of the uhi being struck with mallets, the pigment, made of charred caterpillars mixed with fat, blending with their skin, which was now grooved, hammered into like bark with rich dark ink, the body permanently emblazoned, signed not with the cross, but with the fossil.

Descending from the trees with rollicking gaiety, a troop of monkeys entered the greater playing field and approaching player one from a multitude of directions, to his great consternation, began stealing his rocks, which they cast about the mountain, throwing them here and there, dispersing them far *&* wide, until, in a wild burst of laughter, they knocked down the remainder of his wall, over which he could do nothing but lament, even, at one point, bursting into a slight guffaw, for who can contest a tribe of monkeys, and who can keep from laughing before their antics?

As the sound of the cascading rocks ricocheted through the air, a monkey leapt into the lap of player one, who was sitting before the chessboard, and touched square 8C, activating the fifth film, events of the earth dictated by phantasms, wars of illiterate prophets shaping and mutilating human civilization, the earth in the stranglehold of metaphysics for centuries, todo modo, the despotic militaristic-spiritualism of the Latin Church, blood *&* warfare masqueraded as a journey *&* pilgrimage, the tyranny and terror of the *cruce-signatus*, the way of the cross crossing the seas and devastating all terrain, crossing the globe like a pestilence, a voiding X turned upright to conceal its annihilatory character, vehement incursions into the outre-mer, the annihilation of pagans, the annihilation of Provençal literary and chivalric culture, the annihilation of the dynasties of the Counts of Toulouse and the Trencavels, the murder of the culture of the gai saber, the savage bloodlust of the Catholic Empire *&* St. Dominic's Inquisition, Rome vs. Judea *&* Islam, Judea *&* Islam vs. Rome, give us the blood of Christ, give us the blood of our enemies, like vampires, we savor blood — the bewitchment of theological chloroform, the terror of theological nerve gas, the horror of theological genocide. Triple X.

Devastated by the unending spectacles of the metaphysicians, even player one was too broken to laugh before them, his gaiety neutralized by the darkest of humors.

Taking a rock from his pocket, player two handed it to his opponent and as he took hold of it, the one usually overcome with jollity crouched down, as did the tigers and apes, and the two players caressed the rocks in their hands, rubbing them again and again, everything around them seeming like stone, as obdurate, as dead, as apparently permanent, while in their stillness, in their state of absolute motionlessness, breath hardly detectable, even the tigers and monkeys and apes seemed like stone, dead artifacts fated to extinction, a radically hastened and engineered annihilation.

Gazing back at the chessboard, the film began to grow indistinct, a furious, blinding blur & whorl of images that swiftly went blank, becoming nothing but repeating bursts of flickering colored light, blinking stroboscopically at vertiginous speeds, then giving out, expiring, as if light had been annihilated from the projecting square & a total darkness enveloped the entire playing field, obscuring the events of history, rendering the players and even the animals unconscious.

Opening its wings to fly, instead of soaring into the sky & pursuing an open path, disoriented, the owl fell to the ground with a weighty thud, tumbling about like waste until, entombed within its wings, its irises contracted, sinking deeper and deeper within the organ of the eye, spiraling inward to a dissolving point, its visual orbs gone completely black, resembling rough, glassy volcanic rock, their surfaces grooved with short, jagged, broken lines.

Emerging from the catatonia, player one awakened slowly, dazed as if having endured a paralyzing anesthetic. Not knowing whether it was night or day, in a darkness without sun or moonlight, in a darkness devoid even of starlight, before a sky blacker than any he had ever seen, he struggled to survey the playing field, to condense and organize all of the events that they had witnessed, a history carved by the species, a history it mistook as an inevitability, the 'spirit' of history.

Extending his arms outward before a welter of bewildering objects, the scent of the sea awakened his other senses while he groped at the ground before him, touching whatever was within his vicinity, his eyes starting to accustom themselves to the absence of light, discerning objects here & there, the first being a large rock, which he picked up & clasped in his arms, carrying it with him as he walked to the chessboard.

In a trance-like state, disembodied but lucid, with a swift, sharp movement, he advanced a bishop, seizing one of his opponent's horses in the action, its bones breaking through its scarred, blood-spattered flesh. With a flick of his wrist, he cast the disfigured piece to the ground as if administering whipblows to the disincarnate body of a slave.

As player two awoke, he relished the darkness, collecting & pocketing more stones while, lamenting, he advanced toward the chessboard, his movements slower and slower with each step, laden by the increasing weight he was taking on, till, finally, somnolent, stupefied, as if himself an immense boulder that could only be moved by a multitude of people, he touched square 1D, activating the sixth film, manifest genocide, a bouquet of toxins blanketing the land, territorializing it: triumph through disease, the black soap of smallpox, bloodied Pieces of Eight scattered everywhere, scalps dispersed like broken leaves in autumn, brains knocked out, bellies sliced open, children rifle-butted, bodies mutilated, infernal gibbets of burned, ashen Indians, the holy trinity: the gift of syphilis, dysentery, and malaria, encomienda & the tyranny of conversion, the searing *cruce-signatus* flaring forth again, its terrifying X x'ing people out, whipped & bound slaves affixed to juniper trees, visible through ports, a pagan earth mutated into a protestant prison, flesh for rubber, flesh for gold, wombs involuntarily sterilized, trophies of human fetuses & amputated genitalia, *Kill and scalp all, big & little; nits make lice!*, golden land cleansed of tribe upon tribe, from the Piscataway to the Algonquin, human and bison carcasses amassing interminably, paralleling the crashing of waves upon land, an infinite mass of unending bludgeoned *&* battered bones, *give us this day our daily bread...*

Lifting his hand with great difficulty, as if struggling to emerge from the cataclysm of human and animal bones, his brow deeply furrowed, cut with searing lines of consternation, player two looked down at the mutilated horse, turned to the chessboard, enacted the next move of the game, thereby advancing into oblivion, opening toward an abyss, his body beginning to convulse, overcome with wave upon wave of spasms of discombobulating grief.

Cradling the large rock in his hands like a globe, as his companion was beset with tremors, player one stood before the chessboard analyzing all the moves that had been enacted, thinking out the multitude of possible outcomes, of what humanity convinced itself was inevitable, a teleological or technologically engineered thrust, not a manifest destiny, but a forged one, subconsciously contrived as fate, Hegelian prestidigitation, his mind reeling, his senses abuzz, the synapses in his body pulsing with telluric energies, the catena of films of the decline *&* fall of the human empire whirling through his mind as he peered into the voided sky, *&* in the pervasive darkness, in the absolute pitch-blackness of time, an incandescent Boreal display emerged, though not pastel, but lavic, infernal, extending to the edge of the sky, spreading outward, appearing to come under the earth too, as if the entire planet were about to be engulfed in flames, & before this 'proclamation' of the sky on fire, he dropped the rock on the ground, sat before the adjacent chess-board, yet instead of touching any single square on its playing field, with a wicked grin, he placed both of his hands just above it and, like a pianist playing only enharmonic keys, touched a series of points between the array of squares, playing one after another, activating a blitzkrieg of multiple films, all of which simultaneously emerged in the darkness, manifesting, visible in the air around them, a veritable phantasmagoric history of all the events of the earth from the 16th century onward, from continent to continent, decade through decade, an illimitable series of wars, political purges, and concentration camps, the frenzied surge of industry, the hysterical tsunami of capitalism, the siliconizing of all of space and time, like molten lava bursting out of volcanoes, each cataclysm punctuated with exclamations of nuclear & ecological disasters, the dung parade gone mad, the species the Caligula of the earth, the barbed wire of the animal, plant, fungi, protist & monera kingdoms, the large rock at the feet of player one cracking open to reveal the owl awakening, struggling to extend its oil-drenched wings, shaking them violently, in contest to free itself, the bird chemically aglow, a horrid mutation, its eyes digital lights, wires bursting from its body, microchips affixed to its brain, it shrieking, its voice a piercing howl, the pieces on the adjacent chessboard moving in swift succession, artificial intelligence acting upon programmed volition, one piece usurping the other, till the multitude of films dissipated with the instantaneity of light being sucked into a black hole, leaving the entire field of the chessboard empty, the playing field scarred, a devastated hieroglyph of the earth, its music gone mute, its muses decimated, the promethean holocaust reaching its annihilatory conclusion.

Darkness having closed in, the events of all of time obscured, a malevolent, kaleidoscopic blur incapable of being organized, to the whistling of the wind, the roaring of the sea, & the sudden cracking of a tree, player one wandered about the playing field, gathering mushrooms as the fires of the Borealis continued to wildly flicker at the edges of the horizon, extending in every direction, visible as far as the naked eye could see.

Taking what he had collected, player one dug a hole in the earth, lined it with the fungi, placed the owl within it, then surrounded it with more mushrooms, until it was entirely encased in them.

With others of his kind, who each emerged from the mountain, after constructing a fire, a circle of alternating sexes was formed, with them interlocking fingers, and while keeping both feet together, they shuffled slowly to the left, player one keeping time to the dance with a mournful, wailing chant, while one female mimicked it, moving in the opposite direction, shaking a bowl-shaped rattle in rhythm to the movements, all while singing numerous songs, songs revealed to the individual dancers in dreams.

When a hypnotic state was induced in some dancers, one would break forth from the circle waving a feather for the other to watch, & songs with faster & faster rhythms were sung to propel the dancer into a trance, alternating lines repeating like mantras, until the dancer in the trance state experienced visions & the shimmering, shifting fiery lights of the Borealis flickered forth with ever more intensity — from the mountain, it appeared as if everything was in flames, as if the world was being burned up and made over again.

Rising from the hole, its wings cleansed of oil, the fungal mycelia having consumed all of the toxins the owl had bioaccumulated, no longer glowing but free of all digital encumbrances & flush with the natural bloom of its own feathers, the bird extended its wings and above the elemental order, in the midst of sandstone & granite, of rock-ledges, peat-bog, and forest, it flew to its crag, turning its head to and fro 360°, scanning all of space-time as the blazing colors of the Borealis grew yet more intense and the vibratory resonances of the waves touched the mountaintop, the radiant science of the real, the sea, the shore, planets spinning in the distance, stars coursing through space, all free of consciousness, all interwoven, the owl vocalizing, *hoo-h'HOO, hoo-h'HOO ~*

There it was, in plain sight, the enigmatic phenomenon of the eerie supersonic frequency that first appeared between astronomical twilight and dawn and which was visible only to the Dragonflies, Pied Flycatchers, & Calliphoridæ. What the human could perceive only as steady light, or as a seemingly steady object, or as an eerie and deafening noise, if at all, was in fact a real entity undergoing metamorphosis at an extreme velocity, as if the earth itself began revolving at an infinitely faster speed, directing all of its energy toward this entity alone. With each incarnation, or each perception of it on the part of the insects and birds, for every moment of its manifestation in continents around the world was not witnessed, the entity appeared and disappeared with equal rapidity, vanishing as if eons of time were bringing it in and out of further development.

In the face of the cluster of the bright metallic silver-blue abdomens scintillating in the sun, when seized by that play of dark iridescent vittæ, unbeknownst to her, the entity was captured in media when she began filming what the Calliphoridæ could perceive with their naked eyes but she could not. As the condensed block of insects burst apart into a chaotic spray, she turned her camera to the dark, shifting, indistinct, blurry mass, filmed it zooming over the terrain like a photon bolting from a laser, yet it was not in fact a hologram, fata morgana, or computerized projection.

After obsessively watching the film over and over again, perplexed, unnerved, on the verge of dissociation, the woman decided to reduce its playback speed exponentially.

With each decrease of its speed, as she slowed the film down further & further, its different elements started to break down, the images becoming like still frames in a cartoon, or painted backdrops, as if matter itself was freezing, or cracking apart, with the hovering Calliphoridæ becoming slow dancing entities whose balletic movements betrayed an atonal choreography.

Sound too was highly distorted, coupled as it was with the inexplicable noise of the metamorphosis itself, a clamor that resembled an immense whirring machine operating at Mach speed, or millions of amplified bees, the sound elongated, reaching points of maximum atomization, then breaking apart, where sound was almost no longer sound, no longer a continuous, unified current of notes, but discrete, ruptured points of noise — broken, indecipherable Morse code hitting the tympanum like a battery of needles.

At first transfixed by the behavior of the insects, transfixed by the way in which they separated, intermingled, then finally burst apart, caught in the mesmeric force of their rhythm, she would play the film back to watch only them. Yet, in the cluster of their bright metallic silver-blue abdomens, which became a reflecting shield or mirror, she started to discern images of a continuously changing figure in motion. To study it in detail, she kept reducing the speed of the film until the Calliphoridæ reached a pace where she could follow their movements with ease, tracing out with her eye each wild and chaotic arc, following one, then another, as if each were a disparate musical phrase, interacting with other notes, then bounding off on isolated vectors. And with each further reduction in speed of the film, the insects eventually began to move in extreme slow motion, till they ceased to move altogether and became absolutely still, like specks of paint affixed to the sky, or isolated images in a flip book, broken off from the flow of time like notes flying from a stave, moving into an upper hemisphere, into altissimo ranges, overtones outside the normal range of an instrument, and it dawned on her to not only substantially reduce the speed of the film, but to run it backwards, to painstakingly move through it frame by frame, and as time was being undone, in its severe reversal, while the background started to blur and wash out to the point of smearing, as if civilization itself were being wiped away, in this backward movement of images, something hidden, or hitherto invisible to her eye, was revealed — the dark, blurry mass speeding over the terrain finally came into focus, became visible to the pace of the human perceptual apparatus, became a clear, distinct, and perfectly defined form whose body & metamorphosis she could perceive, and it terrified her, sent a shudder through her entire nervous system, making her tremble and shake. Yet, what she didn't discern was that, beyond the event itself, with each repetition of the film, the sonic vibration of the metamorphosis itself was having a surreptitious effect upon her central nervous system.

In the midst of the shock, not sure she was seeing what she was seeing, her body in a gradual state of discombobulation, she played the film back again & again, looping it so that it repeated without pause, reducing its speed incrementally, moving through it frame by frame, till she could examine in precise detail each movement of the figure and the metamorphosis it was undergoing. As much as the truth of the event unsettled her, as much as its images entered her eyes, its acoustic wavelengths entered her pores, moved inside her body, the sound a vibration penetrating her auditory canals, touching her synapses, touching the flesh of her brain, permeating her cortex.

Shock waves coursed through her spinal cord as if she had been struck with a lightning bolt, inciting convulsions in her body, as if it sought to protect itself from a horror it could not endure, or did not wish to countenance & sanction, knocking her to the ground.

When she awoke from the psychological cataclysm, she was still trembling, her body pulsing violently as if an electrical charge were continuing to ripple through it.

Fighting the torsional force, she struggled to still the spasms threatening to overtake her, her limbs jerking, twisting, shaking, her body an increasingly estranged entity taken over by a foreign force.

Gaining a semblance of control, she stood up, compelled to see if what she saw was actually what she saw and not some delirium, not a hallucination born of insomnia, isolation, or contagion.

Silenced, not only unable to speak but unable to form words in her mind, bereft both physically and mentally of language, muted as if even the sounds of her body had altogether ceased, she watched as she witnessed in reverse movement the mutating entity of an ape undergoing evolution at supersonic speed, *eons of time unfolding in seconds, in reverse time-lapse, from its future to its past, through every state of metamorphosis, as if, returning to the near-end of the Miocene epoch, at the point where homo sapiens and apes had diverged, nature, or the earth, spurred into further development not all species on earth,* but strictly the ape, *which shot across the globe like an arrow of time, millions of years or more unfolding in a flash, a spark exploding in the cosmos, the creature evolving beyond every other species, all of which were left at their existing stages, as if a single element of a future epoch converged with a preexisting one, epochs crashing together in a cosmic mishap or tangle of time, eons folding upon eons, a Mobius strip of histories.*

When running the film forward to watch the ape's evolution in slow motion, as she was reaching the end of the footage she shot and new tremors continued to ripple through her body, as the ape zoomed over the terrain, separate from the sound of the metamorphosis itself, she could make out what resembled a series of phrases, a pronouncement of a kind, but at whatever speed she played the film back, whether she sped it up or slowed it down, although it was clear to her that something was being said, it was too distorted to decipher, and she couldn't discern if it was something spoken by the apes, or something spoken by someone else in their vicinity but not visible in the film, or something which had yet another source, or a sound which, through repeated playback, began to lose its integrity & so disintegrated. Intermixed as it was with the sonic terror of the 300 Hz flagellar vibrations of the Calliphoridæ only made deciphering the phrases more difficult than decoding the riddle of a Sphinx.

In playing the film back one more time, she had the uncanny sensation of the pronouncement being uttered inside of her body, as if through repeatedly viewing the film, her body began to incorporate not only the sonic vibrations of the insects, but the sonic vibrations of the apes. What she heard wasn't however any lan-

guage that she knew, understood, or could discern as a language ——————— it was more a kind of palpable mist that permeated her corpuscles & which she did not understand but harkened to in an alien way, bodily, beyond linguistics, beyond rational cognition, a phenomenal ablauting of a kind, an offsounding into a form of interspecies communication where what was being conveyed was well-defined but could not be articulated in her mind or formed by her tongue, could not take shape in her larynx, could not become thought proper to her body, and as the mist permeated her, flowed through her veins as if some new form of blood and entered her ventricles, her body began to mutate, to undergo metamorphosis, her vocal chords changing, her ribcage taking on new shape, her limbs altered, her skull expanding, her mind mutating, her vision transfigured, her chrysalized from a homo sapiens into a new breed of ape.

In the fathomless darkness, under the flickering fiery light of the Borealis, which continued to manifest, flaring out intermittently, while the players descended the mountain with their cohorts, near the edge of the sea, flies, dragonflies, and bees each congregated in their separate but interpenetrating worlds. No single reality was ultimate or primary, and each broke into and disrupted the other in diverse ways, reality less a distinct, single entity and more something processual and ever-shifting, each insect perceiving an aspect of it the other could not, yet its entirety remained ultimately unfathomable, a dark enigma.

When the players et alia reached the sea, all of the books they had gathered from around the world were dispersed, scattered at the shoreline as the susurrating water flowed in from beyond, an ever-recurring ebb and flow whose gentle music sounded in the air. In the darkness, the scintillating, phosphorescent light of the Noctiluca would shimmer forth and illuminate passages from the books, the sea first washing over the words *fear, dread, beast, earth, fowl*, and *fishes of the sea*, just as it washed over the words *into your hand are they delivered*, the salt corroding the book, entering its spine, infiltrating the pores of its pages, salting them, the words beginning to run, to lose shape and form, the letters one by one changing from words to liquid, mere ink evaporating in the sea, and the Noctiluca shimmered forth again and illuminated the words *intellectual, rational*, and *soul*, which the sea washed over, just as it washed over the words *peculiar to man*, the salt corroding the book, entering its spine, infiltrating the pores of its pages, salting them, the words beginning to run, to lose shape *&* form, the letters one by one changing from words to liquid, mere ink evaporating in the sea, while the animals in the vicinity, in perfect concord with their instincts, in perfect concord with their habitats, lived by the intelligence of their bodies, free of irrationality, free of anxiety, free of psychological complexes, free of mind-forg'd manacles, and the Noctiluca shimmered forth again and illuminated the words *day, thief, disappear*, and *roar*, which the sea washed over, just as it washed over the words *destroyed by fire, and the earth and everything done in it will be laid bare*, the salt corroding the book, entering its spine, infiltrating the pores of its pages, salting them, the words beginning to run, to lose shape and form, the letters one by one changing from words to liquid, mere ink evaporating in the sea, the Borealis flaring forth above while the Noctiluca shimmered forth again and illuminated the words *rite, sacrifice, Name*, and *pronounce*, which the sea washed over, just as it washed over the words *He has provided for them*, the salt corroding the book, entering its spine, infiltrating the pores of its pages, salting them, the words beginning to run, to lose shape and form, the letters one by one changing from words to liquid, mere ink evaporating in the sea, *&* the Noctiluca shimmered forth again and illuminated the words *beasts, speak, automata, & without*, which the sea washed over, just as it washed over the words *a clock,* *which is made up of only wheels and springs*, the salt corroding the book, entering its spine, infiltrating the pores of its pages, salting them, the words beginning to run, to lose shape and form, the letters one by one changing from words to liquid, mere ink evaporating in the sea, while mankind, their actions rarely voluntary and operant but more involuntary and reflexive, became cyborgs increasingly devoid of will, and the Noctiluca shimmered forth again and illuminated the words *possession, private, property*, and *without*, which the sea washed over, just as it washed over the words *essential difference between men & beasts*, the salt corroding the book, entering its spine, infiltrating the pores of its pages, salting them, the words beginning to run, to lose shape and form, the letters one by one changing from words to liquid, mere ink evaporating in the sea, as insects in the vicinity defined their territory, bark beetles released repellent pheromones and emitted acoustic signals, ant colonies maintained territory through marking their foraging trails with chemical signals, every biochore colonized by similar biota, and the Noctiluca shimmered forth again & illuminated the word *man*, which the sea washed over, just as it washed over the words *laughing animal*, the salt corroding the book, entering its spine, infiltrating the pores of its pages, salting them, the words beginning to run, to lose shape and form, the letters one by one changing from words to liquid, mere ink evaporating in the sea, the high-pitched whoops, cackles, and groans of the hyenas, which shifted from soft *&* subtle purrs to loud yelps, provoking unruly fits of laughter in the players, and the Noctiluca shimmered forth again *&* illuminated the word *man*, which the sea washed over, just as it washed over the words *tool-making animal*, the salt corroding the book, entering its spine, infiltrating the pores of its pages, salting them, the words beginning to run, to lose shape and form, the letters one by one changing from words to liquid, mere ink evaporating in the sea as the chimpanzees in the distance searched for twigs, picking ones with the right length, diameter, *&* flexibility, then pruned them of leaves *&* side-branches to go termite fishing, and the Noctiluca shimmered forth again *&* illuminated the words *pride, know, constitution*, and *religious*, which the sea washed over, just as it washed over the words *the gross animal existence of a temporary and perishable nature*, the salt corroding the book, entering its spine, infiltrating the pores of its pages, salting them, the words beginning to run, to lose shape and form, the letters one by one changing from words to liquid, mere ink evaporating in the sea, the nearby tigers carefully, meticulously grooming their paws, their posture grand, noble, dignified, their rasping tongues removing loose hairs & dirt from their fur, the oils in their tongues giving their bright, rusty-red coats a brilliant sheen, and the Noctiluca shimmered forth again and illuminated the words *definition, man, cooking, & animal*, which the sea washed over, just as it washed over the words *the faculties and passions of our minds in a certain degree; but no beast is a cook*, the salt corroding the book, entering its spine, infiltrating the pores of its pages, salting them, the words beginning to run, to lose shape & form, the letters one by one changing from words to liquid, mere ink evaporating in the sea as a group of Pheidole spadonia placed some prey on the bellies of their larvæ, which spit out digestive enzymes and dissolved the meat into a liquid they could quaff, Shrikes impaled grasshoppers till their toxins degraded, the taste and consumability of the insect significantly altered, while closer to the water a band of macaques were dipping sweet potatoes in the sea, biting them, then dipping them in the sea again, seasoning the root vegetables as was their custom, and the Noctiluca shimmered forth again and illuminated the words *barrier, separates, brutes*, and *fixed*, which the sea washed over, just as it washed over the words *how slender soever it may sometimes appear to us, Divine Wisdom has ordained that it shall not be surmounted*, the salt corroding the book, entering its spine, infiltrating the pores of its pages, salting them, the words beginning to run, to lose shape and form, the letters one by one changing from words to liquid, mere ink evaporating in the sea, as a parrot that could only speak Portuguese said, *Ha ha, ha ha, there go the generals*, the bird looking from the shoreline into the distance, watching the streams of ink dissipate outward, vanishing far off in the horizon, words no longer words, just molecules of water blending with the sea, ingested, defecated, ingested, defecated, ingested, defecated, changing constitution with each movement through the entrails of a fish and back into the sea, and the Noctiluca shimmered forth again and illuminated the words *where word breaks off, no thing may be*, which the sea crashed over, the salt corroding the book, sundering its spine, infiltrating the pores of its pages, salting them, the words beginning to run, to lose shape and form, the letters one by one changing from words to liquid, mere ink evaporating in the sea, the book drawn out deeper into the water, it being enveloped by seaweed, clawed by crabs, engulfed in clouds of ink ejected by squid, cuttlefish, and octopuses, till a shark swam by and devoured and defecated it, another indistinguishable mass of matter drifting in the depths, and the Noctiluca shined forth in the clearing of the sea *&* illuminated the

words *master, servant, having, & world*, which the
sea crashed over, just as it crashed over the words
*the stone is worldless; the animal is poor in world; man
is world-forming, poverty in world*, the salt corroding
the book, entering its spine, infiltrating the pores
of its pages, salting them, the words beginning to
run, to lose shape & form, the letters one by one
changing from words to liquid, mere ink evaporating in the sea, the book's spine cracking asunder
as a tiger stepped upon it with its paw, trampling it
to pieces, then running into the sea to swim and
play about, the waves crashing over its body, cooling it, refreshing it, delighting it as it swam through
the water, while on land, due to the surfeit of ecological transformations that had been occurring as
a result of the epidemics and the thinning of the
human population, colonies of bees had been expanding, with thriving hives giving birth to young
queens, an erst of bees irrupting into song, emitting a series of sonic signals, the synchronous buzzing & fitful dancing of the insects creating a rhythmic symphony as they transferred pollen from flower
to flower, plant species flourishing anew, the biosphere increasingly vibrant, robust, healthy, the
players and their brethren spurred by the music of
the bees, each wielding a mirror that they had tak-
en with them and entering the sea, enthralled by
the light of the Noctiluca, they began playing,

bouncing the light off their mirrors, thereby extending it, transporting it to land, as if telegraphs of light, sending the luminescence of the sea into the eyes of the menagerie of animals congregating on the shore, the light of the Borealis above flaring forth in bursts, one by one the animals recognizing themselves in the mirrors, player one & his cohorts gathering close together & holding their mirrors side by side to form one giant mirror, them receiving the light of the Borealis as player two and his cohorts gathered close together and held their mirrors side by side to form one giant mirror, them receiving the light of the Noctiluca, each breaking into further groups & bouncing the different lights between them, shifting between the sea & the sky & the earth, creating a phantasmagoric display of light, the different lights intermingling, unifying, undergoing transfiguration as they hit the mirrors and move between domains, the lights of the sea traveling to the sky, the lights of the sky traveling to the sea, everyone disappearing behind the upheld mirrors, only the animals on the shoreline and the play of light visible, a symphony of eerie colors shimmering in the darkness.

Having streamed her film online after awakening from the coma but before undergoing mutation, it spread like wildfire. Those who saw it first thought it was a hyperrealistic simulation, with some rejecting it as nothing but AI generated propaganda disseminated by evolutionists, whereas others asserted that it was disinformation created by the Russians or the Chinese, or whatever government was orchestrating the cataclysmic events and working to gain total dominion of the world, but in the face of the film, to the more rational, the inexplicable acts that had been occurring across the planet were seen in a terrifying new light.

When the librarians recalled the ostensibly hallucinatory encounters they'd had with swift-moving figures that seemed less human and more animal, frightening and powerful entities, when various individuals remembered sensing apes in their midst, or believed that they were seeing flashes of them, & when a multitude of individuals across the planet recalled the flash of fire that erupted in their minds, followed by the vision of an ape and the worm phrase opening within them & taking hold of their bodies as if some strange immaterial host, all of the irreal and disorienting phenomena they had experienced were imbued with an unsettling logic. If reassured that their sanity was no longer in question, that what they thought they were seeing was verifiable, that it had actually occurred, they shifted between states of astonishment, fascination, and terror, for who knew the scale & tenor of what was afoot? Despite the ghastliness of human history, never before had the entirety of the species suffered such mayhem & terror.

Upon further investigation, after extended examination of the notebooks & other evidence that had been discovered through-out the world, as well as first-hand accounts that began to ripple over whatever communication channels remained in operation, it was reported that the apes began to think and speak in other than animal ways — they did not simply imitate the speech of ánthrōpoi as certain other species of animals did, or merely acquire rudimentary aspects of it, but developed yet higher forms of consciousness. Nor did they become human, as if that was the sole evolutionary path into which early hominids could move, but unfolded higher forms of animal consciousness while able to comprehend human consciousness, to speak and read a multitude of human languages, if not perhaps all of them, and to communicate telepathically, to enter into others' minds, to give birth to thoughts within others, to supplant and overtake others' consciousness through indirect infiltration, a kind of remote, ethereal intimacy, what some began referring to as *penetrative cogitation*... Superior potentialities of the brain that humanity had not manifested throughout its evolution took form within the apes, without however them losing the most vital aspects of their animality. What one could discern in the wise, lucid, perspicacious pupils of the animal, all of their telluric sagacity, was alive in them, pulsing with elemental force, free of a millennia of conscience-vivisection & self-directed rage. Acclimatized as they were to sharp, high air, to winter hikes, ice, and mountains in every sense, and free as they were of metaphysics and of ascetic ideals, they possessed a kind of sublime malice & superior form of health & natural gaiety.

To the homo sapiens still in existence, a perturbing question arose regarding the ape thought — was it a virus in the midst of reconfiguring them? The question made their entire bodies quiver, rendering many into jelly-like entities, or pulp, non-compos mentis bags of mute flesh and bone, palpitating heaps of disaggregated organs. If other viruses could break down the immune system and render homo sapiens susceptible to slow decay & death, could this one be in an early stage of its course, resulting in the changing of their chemical composition and the turning of them into apes? Was the pronouncement the woman heard, and which everyone who watched the film now heard, an acoustic form of germ warfare she had unknowingly spread, a wavelength that could tacitly enter the body and modify its genetic makeup, some sonic bug that works in the animal *&* brings about the death of the human? With such slight genomic differences, in altering sufficient single nucleotides, with accurate DNA insertions *&* deletions, it was not inconceivable for a highly evolved species to send homo sapiens spiraling into apehood, or to turn them into malformed bipeds that could no longer define themselves as human. If remembered, it would only be as some once clever beast that had invented knowing, a beast that flashed into existence, flourished, then undermined itself through an endless series of wily deceptions it construed as progress but which was nothing but a concealed drive to nothingness. Investigators did learn that, once evolved, the higher Apes fled to Lascaux and other ancient caves across the planet to conceal themselves without fear of detection, and it was in those locales that, eventually, they began to secret humans so as to study and conduct experiments upon them before venturing into the world, infiltrating zoos, emptying them of animals, and leaving behind dead, scalped, surgically marked subjects: debrained corpses, fleshless crania, et cetera. There was then no biblical apocalypse, nor any cosmological mishap, and there were no Cartesian Cannibals, nor were there psychopathic surgeons or nihilistic sociopaths, but a superior line of higher Apes, whom many suspected of instigating the pandemic. Their notebooks outlined how they sought to learn why homo sapiens were a species that destroyed its own environment *&* endangered itself *&* others, determinedly moving to near and total destruction, a surreptitious form of prolonged suicide. Before the reality of the phantasmagoric evolutionary turn, and the possibility of another species superseding homo sapiens, the human psyche grew exceedingly fragile. As dams broke across world, like arid branches devoid of nourishment, the minds of homo sapiens frayed, the nerves sizzled, the minds splintered, the nerves hissed, the minds cracked, the body burning and blazing out, a pyre leaving nothing but cremains.

Off land, sailors had encountered drifting buoys unmoored from the depths of oceans and seas, while tectonic activity had altered the terrain of many continents and countries, including Jordan, with the middle of the Wadi Mujib no longer being discernible. In map divisions the world over, librarians discovered that the concentric limits of maritime boundary zones had been effaced from atlases, with inland waters, territorial seas, and contiguous *&* exclusive economic zones having been expunged from existence. It was the start of a furtive reclamation of the earth that had commenced during the pandemic, a territorial imperative to deterritorialize the planet, moving from the elusive realm of the waters to the more tractable one of land, to the nebulous domain of the sky, the upper atmospheres, and beyond, extending into the farthest reaches of space, where the touch of homo sapiens did not end, as if the species were an infinite sphere, whose center is everywhere and whose circumference is nowhere, a virus threatening to engulf & destroy all of space-time.

On land, the reclamation began with the elimination of geographical boundaries, first innocuously, with the dismantling or destruction of hedges, fences, and other marking & dividing enclosures, then vigorously, with the full-scale destruction of border stations, observation posts, & buffer zones, as well as defensive walls, barricades, & ramparts, from the dismantling of Vallum Hadriani to the obliteration of the Treriksröset Cairn & the US–Mexican Wall. It was a physical parallel of the trituration of politics, of the dissolution of all acts of statecraft, and it included the demolition of statues of politicians, houses of congress, and courts of law. The trituration of political temples and icons was though incomparable to the wholesale trituration of religious ones. As if coordinated via perfectly calculated strategy, following the incineration of every image & all ritualistic paraphernalia, every single building of the Abrahamic Empire, from synagogues to churches to mosques, collapsed simultaneously, a mass disintegration that was instigated with the extreme salting, the swift, engineered decay of the temples of metaphysics, those guardians of moral turpitude and ecological disaster, those guardians and promulgators of an ethics that had territorialized, colonized, and terrorized the earth & its inhabitants, rendering it a hothouse of death & pestilence. With this, the higher Apes advanced the despiritualization & restoration of reality and renovation of nature. Having read that a pope declared that he would even baptize aliens if they asked, "for any entity, no matter how many tentacles it has — has a soul," for days on end, they could not stop laughing, laughing so hard that they had nearly died, but they knew that they had to sever the tentacles of that empire and end its eternal absorption & strangulation of the multiverse, where nothing was safe from its panopticonic maw.

In the sky, the deterritorialization continued, with all telecommunication lines being dismantled or damaged beyond repair by insects and birds, while in the exosphere, all satellite networks had been sabotaged, were sent spiraling into the depths of space, disrupted from their trajectories by coronal mass ejections, burnt by solar plasma from geomagnetic storms, or drifted into asteroids that pulverized them. All of earth, from its land to its water and atmospheric masses, was being remade a terra nullius, an aqua nullius, while the sky above and beyond it was being remade a cælum nullius. Free of metaphysics, free of mechanistic designs, free of intelligent ordering, the earth, and the multiverse beyond, was becoming chaos again.

When released from the laboratories, the barnacle-imaged and fossil-tattooed subjects felt beneath their naked feet what seemed like beaches of uncooked rice scattered in the vacant streets, but there were no mass marriage ceremonies, and there were no mass births — there were no more births at all, no freshly born homo sapiens that is, at long last, but bacteria, fungi, schist and shale, the material of quasars and pulsars, atomic nuclei forged in the hearts of distant stars, quarks and electrons with the residue of the big bang, insect, plant, & animal life all flourishing anew. Unaware that the cereal grain littered everywhere was the calcified pineal glands of millions of human subjects that had undergone testing by the higher Apes, the disoriented subjects kicked it aside like refuse. Despite homo sapiens being *(dh)ghomon-, as they themselves once asserted, their antagonistic relation to the earth made them more its enemy than an element born of it, with most of the species ignorant that what they were truly composed of lay stubbornly hidden in stones, plants, animals, landscapes, & woods. Unable to speak, the mobile border within them having gone haywire, them now chameleonic, uncertain, precarious, plunged into question, the subjects gazed at their bodies in stupefaction, struggling to make sense of the array of letters & numbers tattooed on their flesh, the wind blowing about fortune cookie-like strips of paper that read, "*The reek of human blood smiles out at you.*"

In the brief span of time before the higher Apes began to disassemble all communication lines and commence with the total obliteration of human civilization, more films of the enigmatic phenomenon surfaced online, for the irruption of higher Apes had occurred in every continent and country in the world, with other people capturing similar instances of the supersonic flash, albeit unaware of the astounding event that they had recorded, for it could not be perceived with the naked eye. Once having encountered the decelerated version of the event the woman had first streamed online, others altered the speed of what they had videoed to reveal the supersonic evolution of the higher Apes and to warn people of their presence yet, in uploading the video and streaming it to the world, they too had unwittingly disseminated the sonic virus.

Not long after each flourishing of evolved Apes, hordes of humans began to disappear almost as if the emergence of the higher Apes led to the simultaneous disappearance of homo sapiens but, unlike those animals, the higher Apes did not procreate in a wanton, profligate manner. They did not suffer from the ardent & implacable madness of batrachians, which, stupefied except when in the throes of a rut, lived hardly for anything save reproduction. There was far from an equal correspondence in number between higher Apes and mortals, and no causal relation between the events had been discerned either since, due to the pandemic, the absence of homo sapiens from the world stage seemed perfectly natural. Further, it was only after observing the species, studying it with knowing, wise eyes, that the higher Apes finally decided to conduct experiments on a mass scale, to examine homo sapiens of every type & age in every country on the planet, enacting the most complex and thorough study control group in the history of science. The higher Apes wanted to engage in what they read the ancient Greeks called *auto opsia*, to see with their own eyes, to directly determine facts about the nature of the human species, about what caused it to behave as it did and, eventually, the grand autopsy of humanity began. Like the woman that awoke on an operating table & felt a needle exiting her skin, legions of people around the world awakened as they were undergoing live autopsies, the dark, indeterminate figures standing over them, the doctors gazing into their eyes, higher Apes who penetrated them with their thoughts and conducted a variety of tests and experiments, including behavioral studies & the implanting of planetary consciousness, concluding their analyses with the extraction of the pineal gland of each subject, perhaps itself nothing more than a Cartesian parody, for the higher Apes had no need of the comedy of the soul. As the flesh of homo sapiens was being peeled open, as they were being cracked like nuts and probed and prodded just as monkeys & other animals had once been, chuckling parrots were heard to mutter, *the tables are turning, hu ha, the tables are turning, ha ha…*

After having studied the species, after surveying its entire recorded history, after cutting, dissecting, analyzing, experimenting, the higher Apes commenced their pranks, pratfalls, & covert jests, engaging in nightly raids, infiltrating buildings the world over, laying the groundwork for their planetary revolution, for they were polymorphic masters of mêtis. In surveying human history & analyzing its socio-political dynamics, the higher Apes could not help but frequently burst into laughter at how myopic, dwarfish, & monstrous homo sapiens were.

Although they did at times achieve extraordinary things, that was atypical, for the species was generally base, pestilential, and ignoble, and it could not resolve conflicts, instead engaging in extreme malevolence, with one faction warring against another, this one persecuting that one, that one destroying another, whether through embargo, colonization, or enslavement, suffocating, strangling, and obliterating other cultures with wanton abandon, each transmitting their biases like corrupting germs from generation to generation, embedding them in their offspring like booby-traps, ensnaring themselves in deadly lockstep patterns for millennia, at war with their instincts, unable to manage them, rampant bloodthirsty savages gone berserk, attempting the total annihilation of others of their kind as well as others they did not believe of their kind, bifurcating themselves from reality, alienating themselves from their bodies, bringing almost everything in their wake to points of extinction, reaching the final threshold where not only they themselves were on the verge of extinction, but biological life was too.

Brought to such an extremity of environmental degradation, the soil, the sea, and air currents all chemicalized, nuclearized from the core of the earth to the upper atmosphere, from the Mariana Trench to the ozone layer, the biosphere began

to revolt against this accursed share, breeding mor-
bidity and increased mortality in it, while natural
selection gave rise to a phantasmagoric evolutionary turn, with the higher Apes emerging to halt
the further growth of homo sapiens. The dream of
an unlimited transformation of any species is pure
chimera, the higher Apes said to themselves; they
will disappear one by one, according to their order of primogeniture, & as homo sapiens are not
the product of a total but only a partial evolution,
and unlike plants, they are far from autotrophic,
with human rationality a dubious provision paling
before animal & plant intelligibility, those insipid
sapiens are hardly the culmination of nature, let
alone the crown of creation. Although, as the higher Apes learned, chickens have the same number
of protein-encoding genes as humans, they found
chickens to be the taster biped, though roasted
fowl hardly compared to scaloppine di vitello, a dish
they relished.

As nature's nemesis, and due to their hubris
and their infinite despoiling energies, the other
kingdoms began their mute revolt against the less-
tasty fowl, acting upon it from within & afar, for
Nature abhors the animal that denies its animality.
Is that, the higher Apes thought, not the vacuum
of vacuums? The most vigorous revolt was however
enacted by the higher Apes, whose dissemination

of interlocking skeletons of apes, humans, and hominids was but one of their more unnerving philosophical jests, while plants, rocks, and other non-human matter emerging from out of the bodies of homo sapiens was a biospheric jest of even superior wit. With the erasure of all territorial markers, then the wholesale destruction of every dominion created by humanity, the higher Apes furthered the revolt, dismantling the physical domains of every state and nation in the world. One by one, the remaining humans witnessed the swift destruction of all of their institutions, of almost the entirety of what they called civilization undergoing obliteration, from its temples of industry to its temples of politics, with the world resembling a devastated war zone, building after building undergoing controlled demolition, reduced to rubble, pulverized to dust, the earth being wholly reshaped according to an ecological logic, according to the logic of the jungle, of atmospheres, habitats, and milieus. The mutiny was preceded by one final satire, with the higher Apes disseminating broadsheets typed on lexigram keyboards, all of which stated,

If because of their very abundance, the various natural products a country yields can be regarded as artifacts of the state, one can say that they may

> *therefore be used, expended, or con-*
> *sumed (i.e. killed) at will. One might*
> *therefore appear justified in saying*
> *that the supreme power in the state,*
> *the sovereign, has the right to lead his*
> *subjects to war as if on a hunt, or into*
> *battle as if on an excursion, simply be-*
> *cause they are for the most part pro-*
> *duced by the sovereign himself.*

Disenfranchised, the threatened species pondered, were the higher Apes not now the sovereigns of the earth?

In the isolation of their homes, there was however no escape for the remaining homo sapiens, and in viewing the film of the phenomenon, the sonic bug took hold, its acoustic wavelengths entering the pores of whoever listened to it, moving inside of them, sound vibrations penetrating their auditory canals, touching their synapses, scarring the flesh of their brains, permeating their cortexes, their limbs jerking, twisting, shaking, their bodies increasingly estranged entities taken over by foreign forces, incorporating the sonic vibrations of the pronouncement of the higher Apes, the palpable mist permeating their corpuscles, flowing through their veins as if some new form of blood and entering their ventricles, their bodies beginning to mutate, to undergo morphogenesis, their vocal chords changing, their ribcages taking on new shape, their limbs altered, their skulls expanding, their minds mutating, their vision transfigured, them becoming not higher Apes, but gibbering ones of lower origin, the sonic virus taking hold & doing its work, the comic conclusion done.

While homo sapiens were never anything more than metazoans, animals with differentiated pluricellules, like sponges, rotifers, and annelids, rare were those who recognized that, and, as grand as it could be, the species belonged to the artizoa series, to the vertebrate branch, to the mamifer class, to the subclass of placenteries, and to the group of primates not far from the chiropter & the rodent. The domain separating man and animal (already a reductio ad absurdum) was no larger than a tiny rivulet a tardigrade could cross; the abyss between man & animal having finally been traversed, their dwellings nearly all destroyed, adapting to the changing milieu, unimaginable fauna replaced the present fauna, and replaced that strange, delirious, frantic species, which was sent into an altered state by way of a sonic bug and rendered extinct, the transmission having been decoded to say, *Arise and fly, noble Ape, what you called evil, move onward, working* in *the Animal, and let the human die.*

It was the first day of the new era and the song of the earth sounded out, the entire expanse of the planet giving forth its music, brooks quietly babbling, the sound of their continuous rushing extending in myriad directions as they flowed over rocks, creating popping and slurping noises when sliding around them, creeks *&* streams burbling on, the frictional retardation of the layers adjacent to their beds imparting effusive motion to their waters, their trains of long bore form waves full of foaming fronts transverse to their currents, the threads of the streams broken intermittently, forming foaming, cusped, tinkling waves, the drumming bellow of smaller and larger waterfalls cascading downward, great rushing noisy cataracts of white water leaping from their beds, also foaming, but more violently, torn to drops by ground *&* air friction, showers of milky water splashing out in conical patches, their rays like sparking shards of steel burned in gas, the descending water finally becoming rhythmic, reaching their bottoms in sporadic gushes, the atmospheric pressure pulsating, trochoidal waves proceeding outwards in all directions simultaneously, like dispersing excitons in search of reaction centers, choppy seas filling with cross cadences as their wavelets dance with *&* into each other, then break into showers of foam, their sibilant, swishing sounds almost sinister, presaging

their roaring exuberance, their rising, mountain-
ous billows bursting with percussive claps, the protean surface of the waters reflecting the sunlight,
creating an iridescent play of sparkling rays, the
depths below teeming with a supreme abundance
of marine life, cracking bolts of cloud-discharging
lightning generating electricity, heating the air to
30,000°C, echoing in mountain valleys, resounding
in space, the atmosphere, the clouds, the sky,
charged with energy, the air expanding explosively,
shock waves booming out into sonic waves, thun-
der rumbling in distances, strike points with separate branches of the same stroke hitting the ground,
other strokes taking divergent paths, connected
& unconnected branches of negative polarity varying in brightness, dart leaders following the path-
ways of preceding strokes, progressing downward
at startling velocities, return-stroke currents rising
to peak values in less than microseconds, tens to
hundreds of amperes surging through the air,
luminous flashes of violet-white light tinting the
sky, an eclipse of greater wax moths singing aloud,
chorusing together, emitting acoustic signals with
the tymbals of their tegulæ while fanning their
wings, twisting one end of a tymbal to snap inward
and outward, the membranes buckling in, snapping back out, generating trains of ultrasonic 300
kHz pulses midway through the upstroke and

downstroke of each wingbeat, releasing volatiles from their glands, the females responding with their own wing fanning as they approach to copulate, because they're up for the downstroke, whilst elsewhere, troops of *Tonkeana*, *Cyclopis*, *& Silenus* macaques grunt, engaging in atonal barks, growls, and shrieks, their communications rich with intergradations, tonal coos *&* squawks, the itch growing strong, the macaques alternating between female and male copulation songs, a call *&* response chorus, at times synchronizing behavior, at others, the females frequently harassing copulations, surreptitiously engaging in them with lower-ranking males, or mating indiscriminately with males outside their consortship, the loud calls of the *Silenus & Tonkeana* and the *krahoo* of the *Fascicularis* macaques acoustically distinct, composed of tonal *&* harsh elements with extensive frequency ranges, the sonic structure of their calls cutting through dense thickets of forest, whereas in mountains, tribes of goats bleat *&* stamp their forefeet, kicking front legs stiffly forward, flapping their tongues, whooping, groaning, growling, *wup-wup-wup*, the does planting their feet, readying themselves for play, the bucks sniffing their sides, sniffing their perianal regions, *wup-wup-wup*, the does urinating on their front legs, the bucks ventroflexing their heads, flehmen grimacing, contracting their lips, constricting their nostrils, wagging their heads side to side, inhaling the scent of the does' urine into their vomeronasal organs, *wup-wup-wup*, because they know that the eye is superficial, the ear proud, taste superstitious *&* inconstant, but smell the most voluptuous of all the senses, and since their genius is in their nostrils, they inhale, deeply, before engaging in touch, the most profoundest and philosophical of the senses, rapidly licking, making quick, continuous pelvic thrusts, and in trees, Pied Flycatchers sing a series of figures, interspersed with cæsuras, some of the motifs repeated in each strophe, which they follow with other figures, but combine in new ways, with no successive strophe ever being identical, a near infinite repertoire more varied than the œuvre of any poet of the extinct, aped-species, the strophe length of the birds changing, their frequency ranges continuously shifting, with older birds possessing even greater song repertoires, while some adopt song figures from neighboring artists, expanding their expressive range, incorporating the poetics of foreigners, the birds singing up to 7,000 strophes per day, song rates increasing during courtship whilst along the southwest coast of an outlying territory, in peaty soil with high organic matter content, stand the large, robust *Cephalotus follicularis*, whose ovoid-shaped rosette leaves arise out of stout and surmounting rhizomes, while pitchered leaves are born of its lengthy, pubescent petioles, the honey nectar of the pitchers enticing insects and ants which, once incarcerated, cannot escape the bayonet-rimmed mouths of the collars of the hairy, deep maroon pitchers — the prey frantic, struggling to flee, falling into the enzyme and bacterial baths within the craters of the *Cephalotus*, soon dying, decaying, the nitrogen from their remains absorbed by the lining walls of the wild plant, & deep within the earth, after the crystallization of host minerals, the fluid inclusions in the micro-fractures of quartz, garnet, & similar minerals release mixtures of H_2O, CO^2, and dissolved salts, elements contained in the daughter crystals of each mineral, dense, pore-filling, pressurized fluids expelled as the grains are compressed together, the rocks crystallized anew due to rising temperatures, undergoing devolatilization, fluid flowing through the rocks, moving from pore to pore, or through fractures, the mineral-filled veins cutting through the rocks, the pressurized fluid lessening their tensile strength, fractures opening, fluid escaping them as they undergo metamorphosis, endure hydrostatic & lithostatic pressures, their mineral assemblages changing in response to new additions, or the infiltration of more fluids, tectonic processes reshaping the geometric arrangement of novel inequant metamorphic minerals through anisotropic pressure fields, some containing slaty cleavage, some schistosity, others displaying crenulated, spaced, or fractured cleavage and rife with striations or cataclastic deformations, while in various regions, short, explosive eruptions broken by long lapses of time marked the onset of volcanic activity, viscous lava cooling in the central vents of volcanœs, blocking gas pressures, felsic magma pressurizing during quiescent intervals, gas accumulating beneath the plug of cooled lava, then, blasted into fragments shot 40 km into the air, lava clouds of pyroclastic matter extend like immense shafts of selenite crystal, erupting at velocities of hundreds of km per second, the gases heating the air, delicate particles of ash raining outward, the surrounding earth blanketed in tephra, the eruptive columns collapsing, dense clouds of pyroclastic debris & gas surging along the ground at over 100 km per hour, basaltic lava flows, fire fountaining, & steam, the furnace of the cosmos in dynamic play, rich volcanic ash deposits intensifying the fertility of the soil of the surrounding earth, which spins at a slightly greater velocity, for it is far more buoyant than it has ever been.

With the total absence of all artificial light, with the phantasmagoric works of that strange animal which had altered & mutated the entire surface of the earth to a monstrous degree being entirely no more, only the natural light of luminous bodies remained — the light of the sun, the light of the moon, the light of stars, planets, comets, et alia. With no back-scattering from dust and air pollution or excessive water vapor in the atmosphere from carbon dioxide & methane, the higher Apes noticed that the sky was no longer a grey opaque blur, but pellucid, infinitely clearer than it had been in eons, and with the absence of light pollution, the contrast between the luminousness of celestial bodies and their naturally black background was no longer washed out or hazy — with the naked eye, the higher Apes could see the shimmering pillar of zodiacal light, the Galilean moons of Jupiter, the arc of the Milky Way, and even more, for the sky was dense with clusters of stars. On earth, the works of *homo perditus* now largely gone, the iridescence of lizards, dragonflies, & Menelaus blue morphos, as well as other insects and animals, along with a multitude of plants, was more phosphorescent than ever, too, more radiant than even Neptune, the planet a festival of radiant & scintillating hues.

When dissolving human civilization, the higher Apes had destroyed nearly every artificial structure that that species had built, save for certain architectural works that they found majestic, and all astronomical observatories across the planet which, following the extinction of the species, many of the higher Apes traveled to. At this juncture in the chronicle of evolution, they wanted to peer out into space-time, to gaze into the greater expanse of the cosmos.

While manning & monitoring radio, infrared, optical, and X-ray telescopes, the higher Apes examined space-time, starting with the nearest planets. From the summits of their high altitudes, before the blackest of skies, skies free of cloud coverage, with low humidity and minimal trade wind turbulence, they had the clearest images of planets, moons, and other cosmic entities — they measured the motion of nearby stars, produced images of extra-solar planets, and tracked stars ringing the supermassive black hole at the center of the Milky Way. Watching as brilliant clouds of gas and dust were circling the entity, whooshing around it at nearly half the speed of light, the higher Apes saw particles racing, colliding, heated to millions of degrees, emitting X-rays, divesting material from neighboring stars, sucking it into its accretion disk, some of it crossing the event horizon, some of it escaping, beams of particles and radiation streaming outwards perpendicular to the disk, highly concentrated and exceedingly powerful streams extending into space, magnetic fields forming around them, collimating massive outflows, spewing matter radially, a flickering, bursting, violent cosmic spectacle of fire more compelling & dynamic than any drama or fairy tale.

Gazing farther and farther away, deeper into space-time, deeper into the past, toward the most distant light, as the higher Apes reflected on cosmic cycles of conflagration, of continuous contractions, explosions, and expansions, they began observing novel star formations, phases of stellar evolution, & exploding supernovæ in the Fireworks Galaxy.

As the core of a star collapsed, they studied it for hours, watching as the shockwave traveled to its surface, tracking its ejecta, noting its X-rays & ultraviolet and optical lights, as well as the shapes of its light curves. When, after reaching peak luminosity, the curves suffered drops in brightness, the radioactive decay powering the supernova made the higher Apes see themselves as but particles within a vast, infinite expanse whose immensity did not frighten but awed them — they did not think of themselves as blind & wretched, nor did they interpret the whole universe as being dumb, nor did they see themselves as being left alone with no light. The thought was incomprehensible. Perplexing. An obfuscation. *No light? No* — there was light everywhere, there were stars everywhere, there were planets, galaxies, and supernovæ too, not to speak of all that remained unknown and undiscovered. Who but the blind could speak of no light? Light suffused the cosmos to such a degree, and the most varied, wild, and mutable and protean types of light, that only the most solipsistic creature could be moved to terror by infinity and long for metaphysical consolation. Staring into the depths of space-time, the higher Apes did not see it as eternally silent, nor did such spaces fill them with dread. What was before them was nothing less than the most majestic, the most sublime, the most enthralling expanse of reality, *the magisterial phenomenon of life.*

Peering yet deeper into the cosmos, after studying the relation between gamma ray bursts and massive star explosions, the higher Apes examined low-mass exoplanets, star life cycles, and galaxies, & in place of silence, in the joyful absence of the logos, they saw music, they heard an astounding surfeit of matter in action, the combustion engine of the cosmos in dynamic play, a surfeit that increased when faced with the impact of dark energy upon the expansion of the universe, & before the presence of dark matter, there was no terror, nor an urge or longing for doctrine, but for knowledge, to embark upon discovery, not to indulge in mythology, not to perish in some teleological terminus, but to found *an auspicious cosmology*. The infinite spaces were not filled with silence, no; they were only devoid of the chatter of a certain type of animal whose mirrors trapped it in a biographical plague *&* blinded it to the seething, enigmatic, fiery symphony of the cosmos whose astrophysical music pervaded all of space-time.

Far from earth, reaching outside the big bang, in what the anthropomorphs dubbed the muteness of infinity, before nebulæ, quasars, supernovæ, and pulsars, the higher Apes realized what that other species could not: exulting in uncertainty. Joyful before enigmas, they laughed as they discovered that the logical, ordered, symmetrical conception of the cosmos was nothing but a grand subterfuge, for no explosion shoots out in an orderly and unified direction. There was no one-way property of time; it was not an arrow, but more of a wild, amorphous, and intractable mist, grenade shrapnel fragmenting in multitudinous ways — subsequent to the big bang, matter dispersed in countless directions simultaneously, radiating outward like spokes from the hub of a wheel, yet there was no fixed hub toward which one could look backward as was believed, for the hub was only a point within a greater tapestry that continued moving, shifting, mutating, a tapestry obscured by many veils that could not be penetrated or deciphered, and as they snapped the arrow of time into fragments, as they saw it splinter and disintegrate, the higher Apes burst into another raucous fit of laughter when thinking that it was once believed that the universe was static and unmoving, laughed with such abandon that again they nearly died, and they watched as membranes waved and rippled, undulating in colliding rhythms, penetrating one another, generating singularities, further explosions, and new universes, each radiating in untraceable directions, spiraling infinitely outward, extending like branches of coral, or adventitious shoots & roots surging out of a rhizome, and so they thought, each transmitting to one another from afar the observation that, *Infinitas silentio repleta non est, quoniam quarcae et electronici per materiam loquuntur. Nunc terram pulice, quae per millenia peste eam consumpserat, liberamus, et eam igni in vitam vindicamus* ~

COLOPHON

HUMANIMALITY
was handset in InDesign CC.

The text font is *Auroc*.

The display font is P22 *Operina*.

Book design *&* typesetting: Alessandro Segalini

Cover design: CMP

Image credit: Planck thermal dust
amplitude map (2018).

HUMANIMALITY
is published by Contra Mundum Press.

Contra Mundum Press   New York · London · Melbourne

CONTRA MUNDUM PRESS

Dedicated to the value & the indispensable importance of the individual voice, to works that test the boundaries of thought & experience.

The primary aim of Contra Mundum is to publish translations of writers who in their use of form and style are *à rebours*, or who deviate significantly from more programmatic & spurious forms of experimentation. Such writing attests to the volatile nature of modernism. Our preference is for works that have not yet been translated into English, are out of print, or are poorly translated, for writers whose thinking & æsthetics are in opposition to timely or mainstream currents of thought, value systems, or moralities. We also reprint obscure and out-of-print works we consider significant but which have been forgotten, neglected, or overshadowed.

There are many works of fundamental significance to *Weltliteratur* (*& Weltkultur*) that still remain in relative oblivion, works that alter and disrupt standard circuits of thought — these warrant being encountered by the world at large. It is our aim to render them more visible.

For the complete list of forthcoming publications, please visit our website. To be added to our mailing list, send your name and email address to: info@contramundum.net

Contra Mundum Press
P.O. Box 1326
New York, NY 10276
USA

OTHER CONTRA MUNDUM PRESS TITLES

SOME FORTHCOMING TITLES

Scott Von, *Autopoesis*
Carmelo Bene, *Lorenzaccio +*

AGRODOLCE SERIES Æ

2020 Dejan Lukić, *The Oyster*
2022 Ugo Tognazzi, *The Injester*

HYPERION
On the Future of Æsthetics 2006–PRESENT

To read samples and order current & back issues of *Hyperion*,
visit contramundumpress.com/hyperion
Edited by Rainer J. Hanshe & Erika Mihálycsa (2014 ~)

 CONTRA MUNDUM PRESS

is published by Rainer J. Hanshe
Typography & Design: Alessandro Segalini
Publicity & Marketing: Alexandra Gold
Ebook Design: Carlie R. Houser

THE FUTURE OF KULCHUR

THE PROJECT

From major museums like the MoMA to art house cinemas such as Film Forum, cultural organizations do not sustain themselves from sales alone, but from subscriptions, donations, benefactors, and grants.

Since benefactors of Peggy Guggenheim's stature are rare to come by, and receiving large grants from major funding bodies is an infrequent and unreliable source of capital, we seek to further our venture through a form of modest support that is within everyone's reach.

Although esteemed, Contra Mundum is an independent boutique press with modest profit margins. In not having university, state, or institutional backing, other forms of sustenance are required to move us into the future.

Additionally, in the past decade, the reduction of the purchasing budgets across the nation of both public and private libraries has had a severe impact upon publishers, leading to significant decreases in sales, thereby necessitating the creation of alternative means of subsistence.

Because many of our books are translations, our desire for proper remuneration is a persistent point of concern. Even when translators receive grants for book projects, the amount is often insufficient to compensate for their efforts, and royalties, which trickle in slowly over years, are not a reliable source of compensation.

WHAT WILL BE DONE

With your participation we seek to offer writers and translators greater compensation for their work, and in a more expeditious manner.

Additionally, funds will be used to pay for translation rights, basic operating expenses of the press, and to represent our writers and translators at book fairs.

If the means exist, we will also create a translation residency, providing opportunities to both junior and more established translators, thereby furthering our cultural efforts.

Through a greater collective and the cultural commons of the world, we can band together to create this constellation and together function as a patron for the writers and artists published by CMP. We hope you will join us in this partnership.

Your patronage is an expression of your confidence and belief in visionary literary work that would otherwise be exiled from the Anglophone world. With bookstores and presses around the world struggling to survive, and many even closing, joining the Future of Kulchur allows you to be a part of an active force that forms a continuous *&* stable foundation which safeguards the longevity of Contra Mundum Press.

Endowed by your support, we can expand our poetics of hospitality by continuing to publish works from many different languages and reflect, welcome, and embrace the riches of other cultures throughout the world. To become a member of any of our Future of Kulchur tiers is to express your support of such cultural work, and to aid us in continuing it. A unified assemblage of individuals can make a modern Mæcenas and deepen access to radical works.

The Oyster ($2/month)

- Three issues (PDFs) of your choice of our art journal, *Hyperion*.
- 15% discount on all purchases (for orders made directly through our site) during the subscription term (one year).
- Impact: $2 a month contributes to the cost to convert a title to an ebook and make it accessible to wider audiences.

Paris Spleen ($5/month)

- Receive $35 worth of books or your choice from our back catalog.
- Three issues (PDFs) of your choice of our art journal, *Hyperion*.
- 18% discount on all purchases (for orders made directly through our site) during the subscription term (one year).
- Impact: $5 a month contributes to the cost purchasing new fonts for expanding the range of our typesetting palette.

Gilgamesh ($10/month)

- Receive $70 worth books of your choice from our back catalog.
- 4 PDF issues of our magazine *Hyperion*.
- A quarterly newsletter with exclusive content such as interviews with authors or translators, excerpts from upcoming titles, publication news, and more.
- 20% discount on all merchandise (for orders made directly through our site) during the subscription term (one year).
- Select images of our books as they are being typeset.
- Impact: $10 a month contributes to the production and publication of *Hyperion*, encouraging critical engagement with art theory & æsthetics and ensuring we can pay our contributors.

The Greek Music Drama ($25/month)

- Receive $215 worth of books.
- 5 PDF issues of *Hyperion* ($25 value).
- A quarterly newsletter with exclusive content such as interviews with authors or translators, excerpts from upcoming titles, publication news, and more.
- 25% discount (for orders made directly through our site) on all merchandise during the subscription term (one year).
- Impact: $25 a month contributes to the cost of designing and formatting a book.

Citizen Above Suspicion ($50/month)

- Receive $525 worth of books.
- 6 PDF issues of *Hyperion* ($30 value).
- 1 tote.
- A quarterly newsletter with exclusive content such as interviews with authors or translators, excerpts from upcoming titles, publication news, and more.
- 30% discount on all merchandise (for orders made directly through our site) during the subscription term (one year).
- Select one forthcoming book from our catalog and receive it in advance of release to the general public.
- Impact: $50 a month contributes to editorial & proofreading fees.

Casanova ($100/month)

- Receive $1040 worth of books.
- 7 PDF issues of *Hyperion* ($30 value).
- 1 tote.
- A quarterly newsletter with exclusive content such as interviews with authors or translators, excerpts from upcoming titles, publication news, and more.
- 35% discount on all merchandise (for orders made directly through our site) during the subscription term (one year).
- A signed typeset spread from two forthcoming books.
- Select two forthcoming books from our catalog and receive them in advance of release to the general public.
- Impact: $100 a month contributes to the cost of translating a book, therefore supporting a translator in their craft & bringing a new work & perspective to Anglophone audiences.

Cybernetogamic Vampire ($200/month)

- Receive $2020 worth of books.
- 10 PDF issues of *Hyperion* ($50 value).
- 1 tote.
- A quarterly newsletter with exclusive content such as interviews with authors or translators, excerpts from upcoming titles, publication news, and more.
- 40% discount on all merchandise (for orders made directly through our site) during the subscription term (one year).
- A signed typeset spread from four of our forthcoming books.
- The listing of your name in the colophon to a forthcoming book of your choice.
- Select four forthcoming books from our catalog and receive them in advance of release to the general public.
- Impact: $200 a month contributes to general operating expenses of the press, paying for translation rights, and attending book fairs to represent our writers and translators and reach more readers around the world.

To join the Future of Kulchur, visit here:

contramundumpress.com/support-us